Contents

1.

Clay into Pots

Clay is fun to work with. It is one of Nature's basic materials for handcrafted and commercial objects. Since ancient times clay has been used in making many of the necessities and decorative objects of daily living. This book will show you how to make many interesting and creative pieces that you will feel proud to display.

The earliest people formed clay into cooking pots, storage jars, and grave figures. Later on, shallow clay containers held a wick and oil for lamps; large containers called amphoras held the wine and olive oil of ancient Greece and Rome. Plain, unglazed roof and floor tiles were made from clay, as were painted and glazed tiles set into walls and floors. In both early China and Egypt, small clay models of houses, granaries, people, and boats were placed in tombs to remind the departed ones of the life they had left.

Strangely enough, the early primitive objects made by widely separated peoples are similar in shape and in their applied designs which used colored clays as decoration. Later on, as designs and glazes became more sophisticated, and as trade developed between countries, clay objects were carried from place to place by ship, camel, and horse along the trade routes. Designs in clay were often copied so that one may find similar shapes and surface designs in both ancient Persia and China.

But through the centuries, certain styles, designs and technical developments have made it possible to identify clay objects according to countries, dates and even particular makers. It was

1

China that led the way in developing shapes and glazes, and the high-fired porcelain clays; their beautiful Tang, Sung, and Ming pottery and porcelains were made long before European potters learned how to make comparable clay ware, and even today table dishes are often referred to as "Chinaware." As manufacturing processes were perfected in Europe, each manufacturer's designs came to be easily recognized, so that one speaks of a Meissen, Wedgwood, Staffordshire, Quimper, Copenhagen Majolica ware.

But there are still, all around the world, individual craftspeople making their designs by hand and firing them in their own kilns, some objects for actual use, others as art objects to be displayed and enjoyed for their form and color. This book will show you how it is done. You, too, can make beautiful objects out of clay and have a lot of fun doing it.

2.

Materials and Tools

The clay used for the projects in this book is a special type that is hardened in the oven instead of in a kiln. This will make it much easier for you to create interesting items. Oven-baked clays are clays made for home rather than studio or commercial use, as they are baked in a kitchen oven at 250° F to harden the clay. While the clay will harden in the oven, the object will never be as hard as regular clay baked at a higher temperature in a kiln. Also, the object will not be waterproof, even when covered with a special air-dried glaze or painted with acrylic paints. For this reason all the pots which you will make from this clay will be for decoration only, not for actual use for food or liquids.

Chapter 5 describes the various types of regular clay and glazes, and the firing process in a *kiln*.

All the clay projects in this book are made using only three different forming processes: hand modeling, slabs, and coils. These are the processes used by potters through the centuries, as far back in time as any one knows, and they are still in use today. And while you are reproducing the beautiful folk-art designs of earlier centuries using these classic methods of forming the clay, you will be learning and using all the techniques so that you can eventually work with regular clays, kilns, and mineral glazes.

Following are the basic descriptions of materials, tools, and forming processes which you will need to know about to make clay objects. As you work, be ready to refer back to these descriptions for tools and procedures.

Oven-Baked Clays

Della Robbia Miracle Clay, a clay that dries to a light tan color. Available in art stores or craft shops or by mail order from Sculpture House, 38 East 30th Street, New York, NY 10016. This clay is sold in 3½- to 5-pound boxes.

Repla-Cotta is a terra-cotta clay, which is sold in 2-, 6-, and 12-pound packages. Nevo 350 is both a red or gray clay sold in 4-pound packages by Dick Blick, P.O. Box 26, Allentown, PA 18105. There are also a number of *air-dried* clays sold by Dick Blick, as well as by art and ceramic supply shops. Check these stores for other brand-name clays.

Clay Slip

Slip is the "glue" of a potter. Plain slip, made from the same clay as the pot, plus enough water to thin the clay to the consistency of molasses, is used to attach "coils" to each other as a pot is made from coils of clay (see Coils). It is also used to attach handles to pitchers, spouts to teapots, a "foot" to the bottom of a pot, knobs to lids, cut-out surface decorations of clay, and to smooth out cracks as they develop while clay is being worked on.

Slip is also the simplest material to use in decorating a pot. Slip was known to the earliest potters and was their only means of decorating a pot with a contrasting color long before glass-like glazes were discovered. Decorative slip is made from a contrasting colored clay, or the base clay with finely ground pigment added. Enough water is worked into the clay to made a liquid which is thin enough to be painted onto a pot's surface before it has dried completely. The slip is used either to paint a design on the pot or to completely cover it with color. After the pot is baked, the surface can be covered with a clear, air-dried glaze.

TOOLS

Tools and the Working Area

To work with clay, you will need an out-of-the-way place with a flat working surface that will not be damaged by clay or water. It must be a place where unfinished clay projects can stay wrapped in plastic to keep them moist, or finished clay projects can be left to dry undisturbed before baking. Whatever working surface you have will be covered with a sheet of plastic (a cleaner's bag is fine) as you will work right on the plastic. A plastic place mat is handy to put on top of the plastic sheet when you are rolling out slabs of clay. You will also need plastic bags in which to store unused clay, and to cover unfinished pots.

Some of the tools you will be using are regular household ones, so ask permission to use them, or buy your own at the variety store. One or two tools are regular potter's tools, and these you can sometimes buy at a hobby shop, craft store, art supply store, or even at a stationery store which sells art supplies. Look in the yellow pages of the telephone book under art, craft, or hobby stores.

Since clay can be messy, be sure to have a bowl of water handy, a wipe-up sponge, and lots of paper towels. And, always wear a long apron when you work with clay.

Cutting Tools

A stainless-steel table knife with a rounded end and a broad flat blade is perfect for cutting clay slabs, as is a pointed kitchen paring knife. A table fork and a thin, 2-inch-long nail are both used to cut designs into the clay surface; a nail, small skewer or toothpick are also used to draw measured lines in clay along a ruler's edge.

Cutting Tools

Modeling and Smoothing Tools

There are two professional tools you will find useful for smoothing and trimming your clay pots. One is made of plastic and is about 8 inches long, with both a flat, rounded end, and a flat, angled, saw-toothed end. The other is also 8 inches long and is made of a thin wooden dowel with flat wire set into each end; one is a rounded loop, the other is a free-form shape with a flattened bottom.

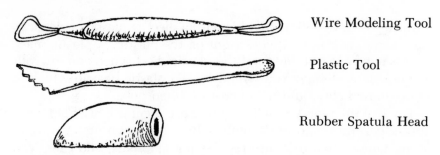

Wire Modeling Tool

Plastic Tool

Rubber Spatula Head

Another smoothing tool, bought in a housewares' department, is a rubber plate or bowl scraper called a spatula. This is a white rubber shape, straight on two sides, with a straight top, rounded at one end. The rubber shape is attached to a 6-inch-long handle; cut or pull off the handle so that you have only the 3-inch-long shape.

Pattern-Making Tools and Supplies

Many of the projects call for paper patterns to be measured and cut out; for these you will need a compass, typewriter paper, pencil, ruler, and scissors. Graph paper with ¼-inch squares is helpful but not necessary. Typewriter carbon paper is used for transferring designs to clay. You will also need a roll of masking tape to hold patterns in place.

Compass

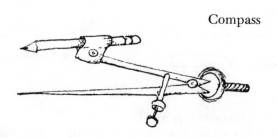

Plaster Bat

This is a round disk made of plaster of Paris and so absorbent that it holds the bottom of a pot very steady. For this reason craft and professional potters use the bats to support a pot while it is being worked on. Bats are often made by the potter, who mixes the dry plaster of Paris powder with water following the instructions on the box; the liquid is then poured into a slant-sided metal pie plate and left to dry and harden. You can have an older person help you make one or two bats, as they are better than tiles for holding a pot steady (see also Tiles, Ceramic).

Plaster Bat   Tile

Plastic Containers

Small plastic food containers are used to hold water, be sure they are large enough to be able to dip a sponge in without spilling the water. By covering a container with a lid it can be used to hold slip.

Plastic Coverings

You will need a cleaner's bag or other large sheet of clear plastic to cover the working surface. You will also want to have a smooth plastic placemat on which to roll clay into a slab. Plastic bags of several sizes are handy and can be used to keep unused clay so it will not harden while you are working on a project. They can also be used to cover an unfinished project so it will not dry out before you can finish it. Tie the top of the bag so the air cannot get in. You will need clear plastic food wrap for covering the household dishes used as molds for slab projects.

Rolling Pin

A plastic rolling pin is best for rolling clay into a slab. It can be bought in a variety store or housewares' department.

Sandpaper

Both medium and coarse sandpaper are used for a final smoothing of a completely dried pot just before it is baked. The clay dust is then brushed off with a soft brush.

Sponges

Sponges are used to smooth and moisten the clay while it is being worked. Cut a 3 × 5 inch cellulose sponge in half, then split one half into two thin ½-inch-thick pieces, so that you will have three pieces of sponge, one thick and two thin ones.

Craft shops sell thin, oval sponges about 2 × 3 inches and ½ inch thick, called elephant's ears, which are excellent for smoothing a clay surface.

Template (or Templet)

A pattern, made of a stiff material such as cardboard, sheet metal, or thin wood, serves as a shaping guide so that all sides of a pot will be even, following the original design. For the coil pottery projects in this book, a template is made of thin cardboard such as the back of a school tablet. The cutout design is enlarged from the diagram for an individual project. As you add each coil of clay, the template, its bottom edge placed on the working surface, is moved around the pot. Push or pull the coil into place so its outside edge touches the template pattern, continuing to check each added coil until the pot is finished.

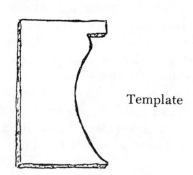

Template

Tiles (Ceramic)

Coil pots can be built up on commercial ceramic tiles making it easier to move pot and tile around without disturbing the pot. A half-finished pot on a tile can be covered with a plastic sheet and set aside. If you have a turntable, the tile can be placed in the center when building up a pot or for a final trimming.

You can use an unglazed ceramic floor tile bought at a home building-supply store, or a glazed decorative tile bought in a variety or department store (see also Plaster Bat).

Turntable

You can buy a plastic lazy Susan 10½ inches in diameter and ½ inch high, in the housewares' section of a variety or department store. A turntable makes it easier to work on your pot. You can slowly move the turntable around and work on all sides without lifting the pot. It is a necessity for *centering* a pot (see Chapter 3, Trimming a Coil Pot) and makes checking with a template much easier (see Chapter 3, Coil Pots).

Wedging Tool

A tool which you will make is a wire wedging tool used to cut a pot away from a plaster bat or ceramic tile. It is also used to cut a ball or chunk of clay in half. The tool is made from two empty sewing-thread spools, plus a 16-inch length of copper wire which you can buy at a variety or hardware store.

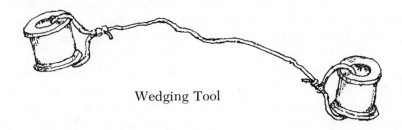

Wedging Tool

Pull one end of the wire through the center hole of one spool until it meets the rest of the wire at the center of the spool. Wrap about ½ inch of the free end tightly around the length of wire so that the spool is held firmly by the wire. Repeat with the other spool and end of the wire.

To use the tool, hold a spool in the palm of each hand with fingers making a fist, the wire emerging between the second and third fingers of each hand. When the wire is stretched tautly between the hands, knuckles facing each other, the wire becomes a thin cutting tool.

Wood Runners

Narrow strips of wood (battens) are placed on the working surface parallel to each other but no wider apart than the length of the roller of the rolling pin. As the rolling pin thins the clay into a slab, the runners will keep the clay thickness even. Once the rolling pin runs on top of the strips of wood, you will know that the clay is the same thickness as the wood. Buy two 15-inch strips, 1½ to 2 inches wide, and ½ inch thick; also buy two other strips that are ¼ inch thick, both sets to be used as wood runners for all *slab* projects.

ENLARGING, REDUCING, AND TRANSFERRING DESIGNS

Enlarging

The patterns for each project are drawn to scale on a grid. The enlarging information is printed just below the lower right-hand corner of the pattern. Increase the size of the grid squares to the measurement shown—½ inch, ¾ inch, 1 inch, etc.

On typewriter paper, graph paper, or lightweight cardboard (for a template), measure and draw larger squares, matching the enlarging information. Then, number the lines. If the enlarged drawing is larger than a sheet of typewriter paper, hold several sheets together with tape to make one large sheet. You can also use graph paper with ¼-inch squares. Count off the number of squares needed for the enlargement, and with a ruler and pencil draw the vertical and horizontal lines. For instance, for an enlargement to 1-inch squares, count off four ¼-inch squares and draw a heavy pencil line.

Now, all you have to do is draw in the lines of the pattern drawing on the larger squares, following the lines on the smaller grid. Draw across each square in the same place, and cut across each grid line at the same place. When you are finished, you will have an exact enlargement of the original pattern.

Reducing

To reduce a drawing—reverse the whole procedure. Make the final grid on the typewriter paper smaller than the original grid pattern in the book. Follow directions in paragraph 3 of Enlarging.

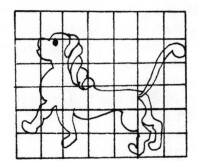

Pattern

Enlarge to ½″ squares

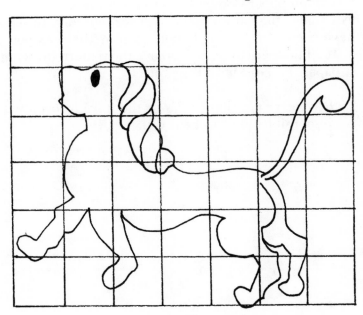

Enlarged Drawing

Same Size

Make your grid the same measurement as the one in the book, and follow directions in paragraph 3 of Enlarging.

Transferring a Drawing

After you have made the enlarged pattern by the grid method, transfer it to the final baked clay of the project. In most cases you will be using carbon paper.

Place the carbon paper, black side down on the baked clay. Hold it in place with four small pieces of masking tape. Put the pattern design on top of the carbon paper. Hold it in place with pieces of masking tape.

Now, with a sharp-pointed #3 (hard) lead pencil, trace over all the lines of the typewriter paper pattern, except the grid lines. You can also use a ballpoint pen. Before removing the pattern and the carbon paper, loosen one or two pieces of masking tape and peek under the carbon paper. Check carefully to see if all lines have been transferred. If not, go over the ones you have missed. If all lines are in place, remove the pattern drawing and carbon paper. Proceed with the project.

CAUTION: Never use sharp tools or the stove or oven without asking a responsible adult to help you.

3.

The Three Clay-Forming Processes

You can make all the projects described in this book by using only three basic clay-forming processes. These are the classic ways of working with clay to form pots, sculptures and box shapes which have been used through centuries by craftspeople.

HAND MODELING

Pinch Pots

Scientists digging up very old huts and campsites have discovered that the first pots were formed from lumps of clay by prehistoric peoples using their hands. Nowadays, we call these bowl shapes *pinch pots*. In making these pots you will learn the quality and feel of clay and how far you can squeeze and pull it, when to sponge the clay with water as it gets dry, and how to smooth out the cracks that develop as you curve and mold the clay into a shape.

Start with a round ball of clay, 2 inches in diameter. Roll a lump of clay between the palms of your hands until the ball is formed, smoothing out any surface cracks with your fingers and a sponge lightly dipped in water and squeezed out. Too much water will turn the surface into a soft slippery mess. Holding the ball against the working surface covered with a dampened plastic sheet, cradle it in the fingers of both hands. Dig your two thumbs into the center, nails and knuckles pressed together, and open a round center hole almost to the bottom of the ball of clay. Gradually widen the hole, pinching and pressing the clay up into side walls ½ to ⅜ inch thick, bringing the walls upward and outward into a bowl shape of your choice. Moisten your fingers with water if they stick to the clay. Even out the top edge with your fingers or with one of the cutting tools. Smooth the inside and outside with a damp sponge. Set the pot aside to dry (see Final Drying and Smoothing in this chapter for drying instructions).

Figures, Animals, and Other Shapes

Primitive people made small human and animal figures from clay which were used in religious ceremonies. Some of these figures were good-luck charms for crops, hunting, or protection from unknown evil forces; some were made as children's toys. All of these shapes were formed by hand, and baked in a wood fire. Later on, more elaborate clay figures were made and in some cases became part of a funeral ceremony in which figures representing the life-style of the departed ruler or wealthy person were placed in the tomb. We have many examples of these funerary figures from Egyptian tombs of early dynasties and from Chinese tombs of the Tang and other periods.

Following the designs in this book, break off a piece of clay and cut and form it into the desired shape, adding small pieces of clay to build up the form. Use the modeling tool and your fingers to carve away clay. When finished, dry the object well before baking.

Clay beads have always been favorite ornaments, and they are made by rolling small pieces of clay between the palms of your hands, either as rounds or long ovals. With a round toothpick make a hole through the center of each one; set the beads aside to dry thoroughly before baking.

SLAB POTS

Basic Directions

A flat sheet of clay of even thickness is called a slab. Long ago, slabs were patted out by hand on a flat surface; now they are formed with a plastic rolling pin and two wooden runners which keep the clay slabs at an even thickness throughout. The slabs are formed into decorative tiles, bowls, plates, straight-sided round or square containers, box shapes with or without covers, and flat shapes for necklaces or pendants.

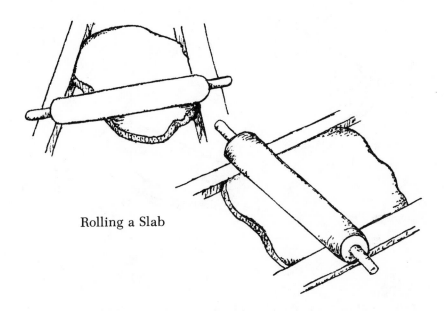

Rolling a Slab

To form the slabs, first place a sheet of plastic (a cleaner's bag) on a flat working surface; rub a wet sponge over the plastic sheet. Line up the two wooden runners (see Wood Runners, Chapter 2) on the plastic sheet; the distance between them will be specified in the directions for the project you are following. Place a thick square of clay in the center between the runners. With the moistened rolling pin, roll out the clay with even-pressured strokes in a clockwise pattern, bringing the rolling pin almost to the edges, but not rolling over them. As the clay is flattened, you will smooth the top surface with a wet sponge and repair cracks around the edges. At last the rolling pin will be running along the wooden runners, and then you will know that your clay slab is now an even thickness. As you work, air blisters may form, but prick them with a pin and smooth out with a moistened finger.

From this basic slab you can make many pottery projects; look in the index under "Slab Projects," or develop your own designs. Following are basic directions for making slab shapes.

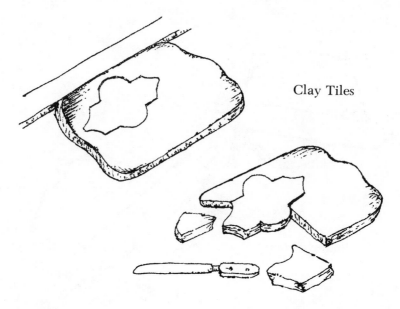

Clay Tiles

Clay Tiles

After rolling out a clay slab, the square or oblong tiles are measured with a ruler; then, using the ruler as a straightedge, cut out the tiles with a small, pointed knife dipped in water. After cutting, carefully remove the excess clay around the sides without disturbing the tile. Allow the tile to dry without moving it, until it can be handled, approximately six to eight hours.

When the clay is stiff enough to handle without bending it, turn the tile over. Using the ruler and a thin nail or the point of the small knife, draw a line all around the four sides, ½ inch in from the edge. Scoop out the center area with the wire tool (inside the ½ inch margin) to a depth of ⅛ inch. This is known as "cutting a foot," and is done to create an air space under the tile to prevent it from breaking when heated in the oven. Smooth this center area with the toothed edge of the plastic tool, the rubber spatula, and a damp sponge.

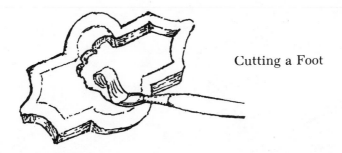

Cutting a Foot

Turn the tile over and smooth the top and sides with a damp sponge and the edge of a rubber spatula. Follow any other directions in the project you are working on. Dry the tile completely, and before baking, smooth all surfaces with medium sandpaper.

Round or shaped tiles. First make and cut out a pattern from typewriter paper. Lay the pattern over the clay slab and cut around the edge of the pattern with a small knife dipped in water. Follow the finishing directions for square or rectangular tiles, and those of the project you are working on.

Bowls and Plates

Shallow or deep bowls, and plates can be made by draping a square clay slab over the outside of a china saucer, plate, or bowl used as a *mold*.

With a length of string, measure across the bottom width of a saucer or plate, or from one edge, across the outside bottom of a bowl, and up to the other edge. The distance between the two runners will be this measurement plus an extra inch. Stretch clear plastic wrap very tightly over the upturned bottom of the mold, moistening the rim of the mold and pressing the plastic against it as you turn the edges inside. This makes a smooth surface for the clay slab, eliminating the bottom ridge or foot on a saucer, plate, or bowl. Moisten the surface with a damp sponge.

Roll out a slab of clay, measure and cut a square 1 inch larger than the string measurement, using a small pointed knife dipped in water. After cutting, carefully remove the excess clay around the sides without disturbing the square. Allow the square of clay to dry just enough to be able to lift it up without it breaking, but

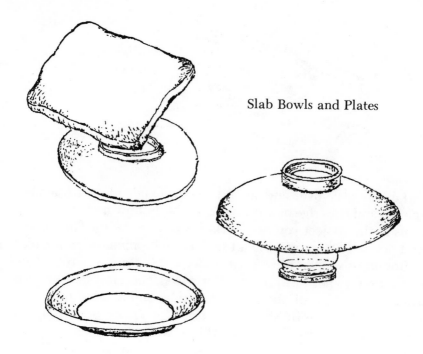

Slab Bowls and Plates

soft enough to be formed over the mold. Carefully lift up the moist clay slab and drape it over the plastic-covered mold. Firmly press the clay against the mold and trim away the extra clay from the edge. Balance the upturned mold on a jar so you can work on the pot with both hands. Smooth the clay all around with the palms of your hands, stroking down from the center to eliminate air bubbles under the clay, smoothing the rim but keeping the clay from overlapping the rim. Finally, smooth and even the rim area if necessary.

Make a thin roll of clay for the *foot*. Curve the roll into a circle of the proper size for the piece you are working on; place the clay circle on the bottom center of the pot, attaching it with slip. Smooth the joining with the plastic tool and your fingers, squeezing the roll with your fingertips to form a straight-sided foot, rather than a roll. Smooth the outside of the pot with a damp sponge and the rubber spatula.

When the clay is just dry enough to hold its shape, remove the pot from its mold; otherwise if left on the mold too long, the sides will split as the clay shrinks in drying. Support the outside of the pot with one hand as you smooth the inside with a sponge and rubber spatula. Set the pot aside to dry for several days, then smooth any rough spots with medium or coarse sandpaper, removing the dust with a brush.

A Round, Straight-Sided Container

This type of pot can be any size depending on the design you are following, and the straight-sided bottle, can, or jar available as a mold. Pick out your mold, measure its circumference and its height with a length of string. Roll out a clay slab of that length and width, plus enough extra clay to cut out a round bottom. This bottom circle will be the diameter of the mold bottom, plus double the thickness of the clay side walls.

Measure and cut the slab with a knife dipped in water, and remove any excess clay. Let the slab and bottom dry to the point where they can be lifted up, but not so dry as to crack when the clay is wrapped around the mold. In some projects designs will be pressed or cut into the clay before it is wrapped around the mold.

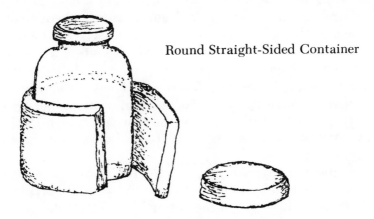

Round Straight-Sided Container

Wrap the bottle, can, or jar with plastic wrap, moisten the wrap, and curve the clay slab around the mold so the ends just meet. Seal the ends neatly with slip. When the clay has stiffened, but not enough to crack as it shrinks against the mold, carefully remove the plastic-wrapped mold from the center of the clay tube. Scratch around the bottom edge of the clay tube and also scratch around the matching top outside edge of the clay round; cover both sets of scratches with slip. Place the clay tube on top of the round bottom and seal the inside joining with slip and a thin roll of clay. Smooth the outside joint so that there is no break between the tube and the bottom round of clay. Go over the out-side and inside surfaces of the container with the modeling tools, spatula, and damp sponge. To reach the lower areas of the inside of the container, tie the sponge to a length of dowel. Repair any cracks that may have formed, and finally even-off the top edge.

Turn the container over and cut the foot (see Cutting a Foot). Set the container aside to dry undisturbed, then go over the sur-faces with medium or coarse sandpaper before baking, removing any dust with a soft brush.

Box Shape

The method of making a box shape from a clay slab is always the same, no matter what the size or shape of the box or square container.

A pattern for the bottom and sides of a box shape is made of typewriter paper, measured and drawn with ruler and pencil, then the five pieces are cut out with the scissors. Two sides exact-ly match the measurements of two opposite sides of the bottom. The measurements of the second two opposite sides are the same as the matching bottom *less* the thickness of the clay walls of the other two sides, as the first set overlaps the other two sides. In other words, if the walls of the sides are ¼ inch thick, then the second two sides are the width of the bottom measurement less ½ inch.

Press the separate pieces of the box pattern against the rolled out slab of clay, then with ruler and knife dipped in water cut out along the edges of the pattern pieces. Lift the paper patterns from the clay; remove excess clay from around the pieces. Allow the five pieces to dry undisturbed for at least thirty minutes, or until they are stiff enough to stand upright without bending, but are not dried out.

When just dry enough to handle, transfer the bottom pieces to a moistened sheet of plastic or a plastic place mat. Scratch all

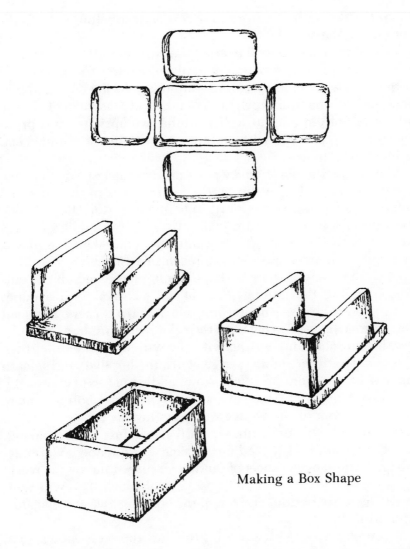

Making a Box Shape

four vertical edges of the bottom slab with X's made with a knife point (see drawing). Brush slip over the two opposite edges that exactly match the measurements of the two second side pieces. Place one matching, upright, side piece against the slip, adding a thin coil of clay on the inside joint. Smooth the coil into place with an index finger and the rounded end of the plastic tool, while you brace the outside with the other hand. Repeat on the opposite side, adding more slip if needed just before putting the upright in place.

The other two sides will overlap the two sides already in place; before putting the last two sides in place, scratch X's on each end of the sides already in place. Add slip to the facing ends and bottom, and put the third upright in place. Add a thin coil of clay on the inside bottom joint as well as to the two upright joints pressing them into position with an index finger and the rounded end of the plastic tool.

Now comes the really tricky part, putting the last side in place. Repeat the smearing of slip on the facing edges of the sides and bottom, then pressing the fourth side in place. Add the thin clay coils to the side and bottom joints. If the box is small, you will have to press the coils smoothly into the joints with the plastic tool, unless there is also room to reach in a finger.

Once the walls of the box shape are in place, smooth the outside, blending the joining areas at each corner with a damp sponge and rubber spatula forming clean sharp corners. Even out the top edge by measuring with the ruler held upright against the working surface, and cutting with the wire tool and knife, then smoothing with the damp sponge. Turn the box over and smooth the bottom so no joining cracks show, adding pieces of clay or slip if needed. Cut away ⅛ inch of clay from the center bottom slab so that the bottom of the walls form a shallow foot.

Let the box dry undisturbed until hard. Just before baking, smooth the sides with medium or coarse sandpaper. Carefully rub the bottom over a sheet of sandpaper placed flat on the working surface; repeat with the top edge of the box. This will completely level the bottom and top of the box. Remove any clay dust with a soft brush.

If you plan to make a cover for the box, then roll out a slab of clay large enough for the cover when you are rolling the box slab. The cover slab can be put in a plastic bag until needed. Once the box is put together, measure the length and width of the box and make a paper pattern. Press the pattern onto the top of the clay slab, then with ruler and knife dipped in water cut around the edges of the pattern. Remove excess clay and let the cover dry a bit. When the clay has stiffened, smooth both sides and the edges with a damp sponge and the flat edge of a rubber spatula.

Measure the top, inside area of the box and, with a thin nail, measure and draw a matching line around the four sides of the top. Make a long, thin coil of clay, ¼ inch in diameter, and attach it to the top with a slip along the inside of the drawn line. This will keep the top from slipping off the box. Let the top dry, and smooth with sandpaper just before baking. Remove clay dust with a soft brush.

CAUTION: Never use sharp tools or the stove or oven without asking a responsible adult to help you.

COIL POTS

Basic Directions

For many centuries and even up to the present time, cups, bowls both deep and shallow, round and tube-shaped containers, have been formed by coils of rope-like clay, held to each other with slip. Sometimes the joining areas of the coils are smoothed together by adding thinner ropes of clay to fill in the spaces. The coils are then smoothed into an even surface with fingers, scraping and modeling tools, and a damp sponge.

To make the ropes of clay, dig out a chunk of clay from the container; the amount depends on whether you are making a large pot with thick coils, or a small pot with thin coils. Roll the chunk between the palms of your hands into a ball, smoothing out cracks or folds to an unbroken surface. Place the ball in the center of a moistened sheet of plastic or a moistened plastic place mat. With the outspread fingers of one hand lightly roll the clay ball away from you, then back toward you in short strokes, lengthening the ball into a rope. As the ball starts to lengthen, roll it back and forth with the fingers of both hands. Gradually shift to the palms of both hands, and slowly move your hands out to the ends where the clay is thickest. Keep the clay rope at an even thickness preventing the rope from flattening. If the clay starts to split or dry out, smooth it with a moist sponge and pinch the splits together. Work the clay to the thickness required for the project you are working on.

The rolling of an even rope takes practice, so don't be discouraged. If the rope gets too long for you to handle before it is the right thickness, cut it in half and put one half in a closed plastic bag; continue to roll the other half. If the rope gets too thin in one place, cut out the thin area, and separately roll the two halves. As often happens, even with experienced potters, the rope just doesn't smooth out properly; squeeze the clay together, form a new ball, and start all over again.

Before starting a coil pot, have all the tools and supplies laid out on a plastic sheet or plastic place mat so that you will not have to go looking for them at a critical moment. Have a bowl of water and a small sponge ready, a small container of slip with a plastic spoon for stirring it, your supply of clay in a plastic bag, a round plaster of Paris bat or a ceramic tile, small kitchen knife, rubber spatula, pottery wire and plastic tools, wire wedging tool, and a cardboard template.

The bottom of a coil pot is a flat slab either round or oval in shape, depending on the shape of your project. Since this is not a large slab, the clay can be patted out to an even thickness with your hands and cut to size with a moist knife around a paper pattern. The thickness, too, depends on the project directions.

Put the shaped bottom slab in the center of a plaster of Paris bat or ceramic tile, lightly pressing it into place. To form a better bond between the slab and the first coil, make shallow, ¼-inch-long cuts around the top edge of the slab. Dip your index finger into the slip and smear it over the cuts, as wide as the rope of clay. Place a coil of clay over the slip, cutting away any extra clay so the two ends just meet. (Place the leftover rope into a plastic bag and close the top.) Seal the ends of the coil with slip, and press the coil firmly into place with the palm of one hand (see drawing).

Base   Attaching First Coil

Making a Coil Pot

The next step is to permanently attach the coil to the bottom slab shape; you will use this same method to attach coil to coil as you build the pot upward.

Support the inside of the coil with two fingers of one hand. Start stroking downward on the outside of the coil with the index finger of the other hand plus the rounded end of a plastic tool. Make a smooth joining between the coil and the slab base, moistening the clay with slip, or if needed, filling in the joint with a thin rope of clay. Press the clay well into the joint as you smooth it, so that there are no air holes to blow your piece apart when it is baked.

To finish the inside, cup one hand against the outside of the coil and bottom area to act as a support. Again, using the index finger of the other hand and the plastic tool, smooth the coil of clay, pulling the clay downward to attach it to the bottom, and pressing it into the joint.

Make another rope if needed to add to the leftover rope in the plastic bag. Make ¼-inch-wide cuts around the top of the first coil, smear the cuts with slip, and add the second coil. Hold the cardboard template against the outside in several places to position this second coil. Repeat the smoothing of both the outside and inside wall of the pot.

Continue to make and add coils to the pot, moving the template around all sides so the shape of the pot is the one you want it to be

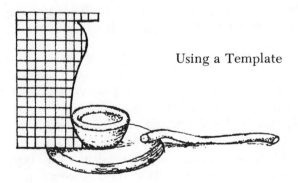

Using a Template

and is even on all sides. Always let the pot settle and stiffen every three or four rows, otherwise the clay will become too wet and soft so the pot will sag out of shape. Let the pot dry for half an hour, then add three more rows. Continue this way until the pot is finished according to the design you are following.

Constantly check the pot, inside and out, to make sure there are no holes or cracks in the clay walls. The sides will have small ridges and bumps but these will be smoothed out when you trim the pot after it is partly dry, a stage potters call *leather hard*.

A pot can be left half finished as long as the pot, unused coils of clay, and extra clay are kept at the same moistness. Cover the pot on its plaster bat or ceramic tile with a plastic bag which will fit loosely over both; tie the bag opening so no air will get in to dry out the pot. Also store the extra coils and clay in a tied plastic bag. Get used to doing this, because if you are adding a supporting foot, a handle, a teapot spout, or cutout clay designs, they all have to be added to a moist clay pot of the same degree of moistness as the additions. Moist clay added to dry clay will never form a proper bond, and the extra pieces will fall off in the baking.

Trimming a Coil Pot

Allow the pot to stand undisturbed until it is leather hard; the surface will be firm, but not hard and dry. Have the turntable, modeling tools, sponge, and bowl of water handy, plus the rubber spatula and the wide wedging tool.

Center the plaster bat or ceramic tile holding the pot on the turntable, bracing either one with four small balls of clay pushed lightly on opposite sides of the bat or tile.

Next comes the very important step of "centering" the pot, so that as you trim the pot all sides will be even. Hold your hand in one place, bracing it on an upturned glass or jar, with your extended index finger just touching the middle of the pot. Revolve the turntable slowly; if your finger continues to touch the pot all the way around, then the pot is centered. If not, move the bat or tile in the right direction and check again; when all is even, hold the bat or tile firmly with the balls of clay. Since a coil pot is a little bumpy, you may not be able to center it exactly, but get it close enough, checking both the top and bottom of the pot for centering.

Hold the trimming tool firmly in one hand, wrist braced on the top of the glass or small jar. With the other hand, move the turntable slowly around, turning the pot against the wire tool which is held stiffly in one place. As the pot turns, any bumps on the surface will be trimmed away. Work up and down the height of the pot, always holding the tool at one level during a complete turn of the pot. In this way all sides will be trimmed evenly. Work slowly and with minimum pressure, otherwise the pot will spin off the turntable. As you work, moisten the surface with a damp sponge if needed. Finally smooth the surface with the straight edge of the rubber spatula and then the sponge as the pot turns. Trim and smooth the top edge of the pot.

If you are making a more or less open-top pot, smooth the inside while the pot is on the turntable. Hold the wire tool against the inside while the turntable revolves, then scoop out the shreds of clay. Finally smooth the inside with a damp sponge and the rubber spatula.

A shallow, flared bowl shape is trimmed on the inside first; then when that is finished, the bowl is removed from the bat or tile, turned over, centered again, and the outside trimmed and smoothed.

When you are satisfied with the shape and smoothness of a pot, cut it off the tile with the wire wedging tool, a spool held in each hand, and the wire tautly stretched. Pull the wire slowly between the bottom of the pot and the bat or tile. Be very careful not to catch the clay bottom and pull the pot over.

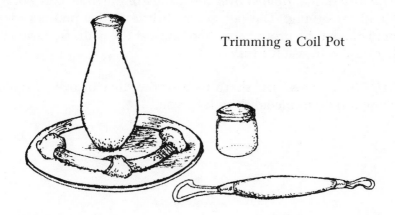

Trimming a Coil Pot

Cutting a Foot

The bottom of any pot, tile, or slab is finished with a rim around the edge, the center cut away so there is a little air space to prevent the cracking of the clay during baking.

Turn the pot over and smooth the bottom. Depending on the size of the pot and the diameter of the bottom, leave a ¼ to ½ inch rim around the outside edge, digging out the inside area with the wire modeling tool to a depth of ⅛ to ¼ inch. Finish this inside bottom area by scraping in a circular motion with the toothed-edge of the plastic tool.

Final Drying and Smoothing

Allow the pot to dry for two or three days on a clean bat or tile in a safe, undisturbed place. If the pot walls are very thick, or the weather very damp, the drying time may be longer. It is best to be on the safe side and allow an extra day or two, as the surface of the pot may be dry to the touch, but the interior of the clay wall may be damp. Any moisture will create steam when the pot is in the oven. As the heat will first harden the outside surface of the pot, the steam, in order to escape, will burst through the outer surface, spoiling the pot.

Air can also expand inside a hollow object in the oven and break it. To prevent this, make a small hole in the dried pot so the air can escape, but make sure that the hole will not be covered up during the baking.

Lightly rub sandpaper over the surface of the dried clay pot for a final smoothing. The pot is very brittle at this point, so you could crack it by pressing too hard against the wall. Remove any clay dust with a soft brush.

CAUTION: Never use sharp tools or the stove or oven without asking a responsible adult to help you.

4.

Finishing a Pot

Once a clay pot has been formed and dried, it is still only in a first stage of completion called *greenware*. The pot has to be handled very carefully as it will break easily or crumble. If, by any chance, it is doused with water, it will return to muddy clay. To take the pot into the next step away from being just dried clay, it has to be hardened by heat. After that it is decorated by solid colors, a colored design, and a shiny *glaze*.

BAKING CLAY

Tools

When you are ready to bake the clay pot in the kitchen oven, ask a responsible adult for permission, and if needed, ask for help in using the oven and arranging the pots to be baked.

Only a few kitchen tools are used to bake a pot made of oven-baked clay. A *baking sheet* holds the pots level in the oven; the size depends on the number and size of the pots to be baked. You can use a heavy aluminum foil pie plate or a shallow oblong foil pan, or a metal baking sheet. All of these can be bought at the supermarket, variety store, or housewares section of a department store. Be sure that the pan you use is clean and free of grease.

You will need a simple *oven thermometer* to put inside the oven on the baking sheet beside the pot or pots. This can be an inexpensive one from the variety store. The built-in stove thermometer will not give you an accurate enough beside-the-pot reading, and this is an important heat measurement.

Tools for Oven Baking

Three thick *pot holders* are needed—two for taking the pan or pot out of the oven, and one to be doubled up, to hold the oven door partly open during baking.

Oven Baking

Follow the manufacturer's directions for baking a clay pot, as there may be slight differences from product to product.

Pot Ready to be Baked

In general, put the pot on a metal baking pan with the oven thermometer placed beside it on the pan. Put the pan on the middle rack of a *cold* oven, leaving the oven door *wide open*; turn the oven heat on low. Leave the door open for half an hour; the temperature should climb to 150° F. and stay there. Adjust the heat if the oven thermometer shows a higher or lower temperature. It is during this half hour that your pot will finally dry out and any inner moisture will be dried up before the outside surface bakes hard. If you start out with a hot oven, your pot will shatter.

At the end of the half hour, almost close the oven door, leaving an opening 1½ to 2 inches wide *all during the final baking.* Use a pot holder if necessary to wedge the door open. Raise the oven temperature to 250° F. and keep it there for the length of time specified by the manufacturer; for instance the time is three-quarters of an hour for Della Robbia Miracle Clay.

When the end of the baking time is reached, turn off the oven, and open the door. Let the pot cool down in the oven before taking it out. The pot is now *fired* and has become *bisque* ware; this is clay baked until it becomes hard but not waterproof. However, the pot will not melt back into soft clay if put in water.

The pot is now ready to be decorated with colored or clear glazes, or with acrylic paint.

COLORING AND GLAZING THE CLAY POT

Tools and Supplies:

Brushes

For air-dried glazes you will need soft, watercolor brushes of several sizes and shapes; broad and flat, thin and rounded with good points. For acrylic paints and polymer medium (clear) you will need nylon brushes of several sizes and shapes; broad and flat, thin and rounded with good points.

Small paper or plastic cups (throw-away types), or aluminum foil cupcake pans will be needed to hold small quantities of paint.

For stirring the glazes, use wooden sticks which can be either tongue depressors, lollipop sticks, or sections of thin bamboo garden stakes.

Air-dried glazes both colored and clear are available in small jars in art, craft, department stores, where the oven-baked clay is sold, or by mail-order from the manufacturer. They can *only* be used on the oven-baked clay of the same manufacturer. The final color does not change during drying. Different manufacturers have their own types of color glazes, clear glaze, hardener, reducer, and in one case an underglaze to seal the clay before putting on the color.

All the soft brushes used for putting on the glazes have to be kept very clean, as do the wooden sticks used to stir the glazes. Dip brushes and sticks in reducer or turpentine and wipe clean with paper towels.

Applying Glaze

Air drying of a glaze takes several days. Rather than one thick coat, use two thin coats, thinning the glaze according to the manufacturer's directions. Drying time depends on the weather, so it can take anywhere from four to eight days.

You can experiment with color combinations as any color can be mixed with another, or a little color added to a clear glaze to tint it. After a color glaze has dried completely, you can decide whether to cover it with a clear glaze for a brighter finish. Or a little clear glaze can be added to the color glaze to brighten it. Each project will list the colors to use on the individual pot.

None of the glazes are completely waterproof, so none of the objects can be used for serving food, or liquids, or as a vase filled with water for flowers. These are all decorative display objects, and the vases can be used for dried or artificial flowers.

Acrylic Paint

The best all-around paint for pottery projects in this book is acrylic paint. It can be thinned with water or acrylic polymer medium for a transparent look; it can be applied thickly so as to be opaque, or as a raised design; it is waterproof, and dries quickly.

Buy acrylic paint in tubes. Use the color directly from the tube, or mix two colors together to form another color. For instance, if you have one tube of blue and one of yellow, mix equal amounts together to make green.

Before starting to mix the paint, cover the working surface with several sheets of newspaper. Have extra papers handy so you can cover any spilled paint with fresh paper.

Since acrylic paint dries very quickly, use throwaway containers as mixing pans—individual aluminum foil cupcake pans are good, or small plastic drinking cups. After putting on the first coat of paint, let it dry before adding a second coat. To keep a special mixed color from drying out put the paint into a small jar with a tight fitting cover. This way, the paint will be liquid for the second coat. You may find that a number of the clay pots will need a second coat of color, as the color has to be thin enough to flow on smoothly, but not so thin as to run off the sides of a pot, or to "puddle" in the middle of a dish.

There are two acrylic polymers that can be used with acrylic paints. One is *gloss* which is used instead of water as a thinner, and gives the paint a high gloss when dry. The other is *matte*, which is used in the same way, but gives the paint a nongloss surface. Both mediums can be used as a final coat over the paint, making for a harder finish.

Always wipe off the screw top and the cap of a paint tube right after using. Otherwise the cap will stick, and it will be hard to take off the tube the next time you use the paint. Do the same for the jars of gloss or matte medium.

For acrylic paint you will need soft nylon brushes, either flat or round, as they do not leave brush marks on the paint. Always keep a jar of clean water beside you when you work. Keep the brushes in the water when you are not using them, so that no paint will harden on the bristles. Wipe off the water with a cloth or facial tissue before dipping the brush in the color. When you are through, wash the brush thoroughly with soap and water. If the paint does dry on a brush, use denatured alcohol to remove it.

CAUTION: Never use sharp tools or the stove or oven without asking a responsible adult to help you.

5.

High-Temperature Clays and Kiln Firing

All the projects in this book can be made with the higher temperature clays and glazes, as the techniques described are the classic ones used by all potters. We do not show how to make a pot on a potter's wheel, because it is an advanced technique requiring special equipment. The high-temperature clays are "baked" in a special oven called a *kiln*, and the baking process is called *firing*.

Clay

The higher temperature clays are fired in a kiln at 1803° to 1940° F. (Cone 07–04) and are called low-fire or earthenware clays. High-fire or stoneware clays are fired at 1915°, 2134°, 2336° F. (Cone 05–3, 9). The low-fire clays can be either buff, brown, black, white, red, or terra-cotta in color. High-fire clays are usually buff or white. Many of the standard clays sold by all manufacturers have the same identifying names such as: Jordan (buff), Monmouth (buff), or Mexican (red or terra-cotta).

When fired, objects made with the higher temperature clays are harder than oven-baked clays. When covered with glaze, or slip and glaze, and fired again to melt and harden the glaze the pots become useable and waterproof.

Kiln and Firing

A craft kiln is a metal box, lined with special, lightweight fire bricks to hold the heat inside, and to keep the outside metal from getting too hot. The electricity runs through coils of wire (sunk

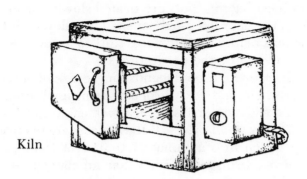

Kiln

into the bricks) like the wires in an electric heater or toaster, creating the intense heat.

The loading door is either on top or one side. There is a peephole in the door's center, covered by a sliding piece of metal. This opening is used to check the heat inside the kiln.

Peephole

When the kiln is filled with greenware, a *cone* of a special clay is put inside the kiln, on a level with the peephole—in place of the oven thermometer which was used to check the heat of the kitchen oven. The cones are numbered according to the heat at which they melt. And this melting point matches the point at which a particular type of clay is baked to its final hardness. When the tip of the cone begins to bend down, the right temperature has been reached, and the kiln heat is turned off.

Cones, Before and After Firing

Just as in oven baking, pots are heated slowly for an hour in the kiln, with the door left partly open. This allows all the water to leave the pots before their surfaces start to harden. Any water left inside would cause the pot to break.

The length of firing time depends on the size of the kiln, the number of pots in it, and the type of clay being used. For instance, a small test kiln will have an inside measurement of 5 inches square. This will hold only small pieces. If these pieces are made of earthenware clay which fires at cones 07 to 04 (1803° to 1940° F.), you would have a firing time of less than an hour, after the door is closed.

You will soon learn how long a kiln takes to fire and to cool. Keep careful records in a notebook—the date, the cone number, the type of clay used, the firing time, how many pots in the kiln, and how long the kiln took to cool.

Kilns that are heated to high temperatures need a long time to cool off. If the door is opened too soon, the pots inside will crack. Do not open the door, *even to peek*, until you can keep your hand on the outside of the kiln door. Then open the peephole to let the heat out gradually. Later still, open the door a little bit. Finally —look in.

Glazing in a Kiln: Slip and Clear Glaze

When a kiln-fired pot is glazed, the glaze is a solid color over the whole pot, except the foot. If a design is wanted then, while the pot is still in the leather-hard stage, a colored or white slip is brushed over the surface. As it dries it becomes part of the clay pot. A design of colored slip can be painted over the first slip coat.

Often, this second coat also covers the whole pot. The design is then scratched through the top coat, so that the color of the first coat shows through.

Or, a slip design can be painted directly on the leather-hard surface, allowing the color of the clay to form the background of the design.

After the first firing, a clear glaze is put on, either by dipping or pouring. In this second kiln firing, the glaze turns into transparent glass, brightening and preserving the design under it. If the slip is white, then after the first firing, a design is painted on with ceramic paints; this is covered with clear glaze and fired. See firing directions at the end of the Solid Color Glazes.

Solid Color Glazes

Solid color glazes are put on the bisque ware after the first firing, by dipping or pouring.

For dipping, a large, deep container is filled with the glaze. Hold the bottom of the pot with your fingers or tongs, and dip the pot into the glaze. Place the pot on a cake rack over a wide bowl to drain. Repair any areas marked by your fingers.

For pouring, put the glaze in an enameled metal pitcher. Fill your pot half full of glaze. Pour the glaze out, turning the pot around slowly, so all the inside is covered. Turn upside down on the cake rack over a wide bowl, and let drain. Now pour glaze carefully over the outside surface. After the pot has stopped dripping, lift the rack off the bowl, and let the pot dry. Repair any unglazed areas, especially around the rim. Pour leftover glaze in the bowl and pitcher back into the jar. Keep covered for your next glazing.

Be careful in handling the pot, so that you do not scratch the glaze. Be sure no glaze is on the bottom of the pot. Wipe off any that you find there.

Fire the pot in the kiln, balancing the pot on a *stilt*, so that any glaze that might drip down will not hold your pot to the floor of the kiln. Glazing temperatures will be marked on the glaze bottle.

CAUTION: Never use a kiln except under the close supervision of an experienced potter.

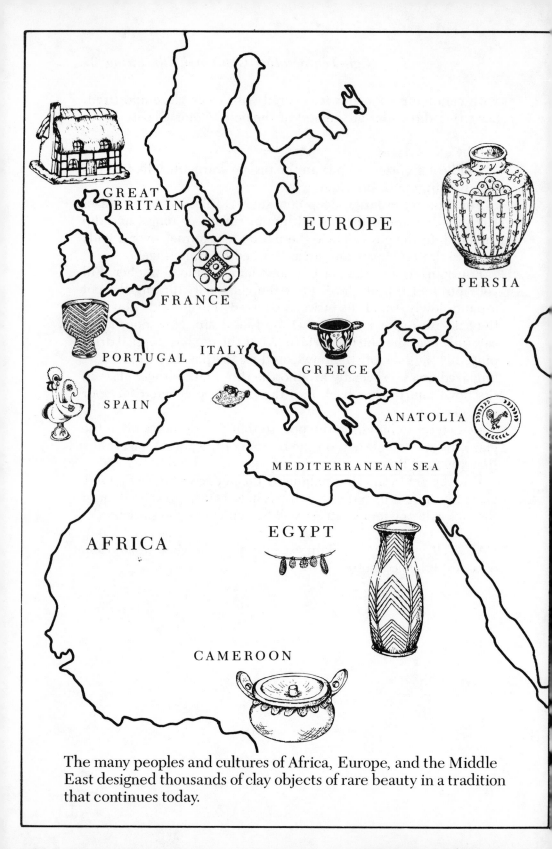

The many peoples and cultures of Africa, Europe, and the Middle East designed thousands of clay objects of rare beauty in a tradition that continues today.

6.

The Projects

The following projects are all based on authentic designs of clay objects from very ancient to just old. All the designs have been carefully chosen for their easily made, simple designs suited to oven-baked clay or even to kiln-baked clay. The designs all reflect the many styles of pottery in those countries where clay work was developed to a highly skilled craft.

The introductions to each project give the background of the piece, and you can put yourself back in time as you make the pot or plate, jewelry, or sculpture. It's your way of creating a time-machine. In the end, you will have a finished object to hold in your hands—one that you have brought back from the past.

When you go to a museum, look at the ancient pottery, and try your hand at making a similar piece. Make a small sketch, and note the approximate size of the pot, and the colors of the glaze or design. Or you may see a clay pot in a book or magazine that you will want to copy for your collection. This book gives you the techniques for almost any project you want to undertake.

Cameroon, Africa

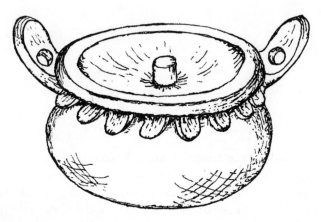

CLAY COOKING POT

A shallow clay cooking pot with handles and a cover is a beautiful shape. It has a pressed cloth imprint on the surface, with little tabs or crenellations of clay decorating the top. The potters of the country of Cameroon in Africa have a long history of designing clay pots for practical uses, from the eight-foot-high grain storage jars, down to small containers and drinking cups.

The project jar measures 6 inches from handle to handle, while the bowl is 4½ inches in diameter. The bowl is built up with coils, with the handles and cover made from a rolled-out slab of clay

Materials and Tools

typewriter paper, lightweight cardboard, pencil, ruler, scissors,
    compass
oven-baked clay, approximately 1 pound
cheesecloth, 15 × 20 inches
tools and supplies (Chapter 2)
clear air-dried glaze or acrylic polymer matte medium
flat watercolor brush—¾ inch wide (for air-dried glaze)
flat nylon brush—¾ inch wide (for acrylic polymer matte medium)

Directions

1. For the coil pot, read the directions in the Chapter 3 (Coil
Pots).

2. Enlarge the template pattern on the cardboard, and cut
out with the scissors (see Chapter 2 on Enlarging). Enlarge the
handle pattern on the typewriter paper and cut out.

Step 2   Steps 2 and 7

Template, discard dotted area

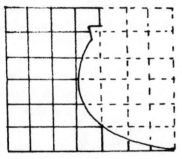

Enlarge to ½″ squares

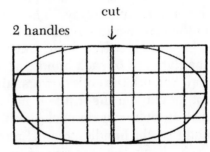

2 handles   cut ↓

Enlarge to ½″ squares

3. Pat out a clay disk, 1¼ inches in diameter and ⅜ thick;
center the disk on a plaster bat or tile. Build up the 2¼-inch-high
bowl with coils, starting on the outside of the disk (see drawing).
Check all around with the template and ruler as you build up the
pot, making sure that it is centered. The top opening is 3¾ inches
in diameter.

4. Finish off the top edge with a coil ½ inch in diameter that extends out from the edge, smoothing it in a concave curve to the edge of the opening (see drawing).

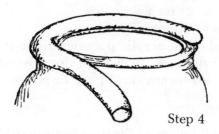

Step 4

5. While the clay surface is moist, drape the cheesecloth over the pot and press it lightly against the clay to leave an imprint of the cloth over the surface. Carefully remove the cloth.

6. Roll out a slab of clay ¼ inch thick, 5 inches wide, and 7 inches long to be cut into the crenellated decorations, the handles, and the cover of the pot (see Chapter 3).

7. From the slab, cut out a 4-inch-long oval of clay (put handle pattern on the clay). The oval handle should be 2 inches wide in the center and have rounded ends. Cut the oval in half crosswise and let stiffen a bit, until it can be lifted up. Next, attach the flat ends of each handle at opposite sides of the pot near the top. Smooth the ends down against the pot with slip and an extra roll of clay on the inside if needed. Carefully cut out a circle ½ inch in diameter on each handle at the rim of the pot. Smooth and ease the handles to an almost upright position (see drawing).

8. From the long side of the slab cut out a strip, ½ × 7 × ¼ inch thick. Cut the strip into sixteen ¾-inch-wide pieces. With slip, attach eight of the pieces to one side of the pot, and eight pieces on the other side—between the handles, and up against the underside of the coil rim, leaving a ¼-inch space between each piece. Pinch the bottom ends together a bit to shape them (see drawing).

9. For the cover, measure the distance across the top at the inside edge of the coil rim; it should be about 4 inches. With the compass, draw the exact size circle on the typewriter paper, and cut it out with the scissors. Lay the pattern over the rest of the clay slab and cut out the circle of clay. Let it stiffen a bit, then form the circle into a very shallow, concave "dish." Measure with the ruler to be sure that it will fit inside the rim, but is larger than the opening. Pot and lid will shrink proportionately. Add a 1-inch coil of clay, ½ inch in diameter, upright in the center as a handle (see drawing).

10. Allow the pot and the cover to dry until leather hard, then cut out a shallow foot or air space in the bottom of the pot (see Chapter 3, Cutting a Foot). Go over the cover, handles, and crenellated decorations with a damp sponge and the wire modeling tool to smooth the surfaces—but do not touch the cloth-imprinted surface of the pot. Set the two pieces aside for three or four days or longer to dry thoroughly.

11. When dry, bake in the oven following directions in Chapter 4, Finishing a Pot.

12. When the pot and cover have cooled, cover all surfaces with either the air-dried clear glaze or the acrylic polymer matte medium. Let dry completely.

China

CLAY BOTTLE

In China through many centuries, household and ceremonial objects were made of clay or metal. Round and square bottles were made to hold liquids, and drinking cups were also made of clay in many different sizes and styles. Glass objects were very rare, and confined to decorative vases in forms similar to clay or metal vases.

For this project, you will make a rectangular clay bottle like one made in China several hundred years ago. This unusual bottle is eight inches high, with two clay loops on the top for attaching carrying cords. Perhaps it was hung from a saddle or a belt during a hunting expedition. The design on each narrow side is done with green lines; the rabbit and the border are in shades of ochre yellow; the tree is green; the background is white. The project design is based on a seven-inch-high bottle.

Materials and Tools
typewriter paper, carbon paper, pencil, ruler, scissors
oven-baked clay, approximately 1 pound
tools and supplies (Chapter 2)
air-dried glazes or acrylic paints,
   white, chrome yellow, brown, green
acrylic polymer gloss medium
flat, ¾ inch wide, and round, #4 and #2 watercolor brushes
   (for air-dried glaze)
flat, ¾ inch wide, and round, #4 and #2 nylon brushes
   (for acrylic paint)

Directions
   1. First read the directions in Chapter 3 for making the Box Shape.
   2. You will only have to measure and cut out three patterns from the typewriter paper for this rectangular bottle (you will be cutting out two clay shapes from each pattern): a. 1¼ × 6 inches for the narrow sides; b. 4½ × 6 inches for the front and back; c. 2 × 4½ for the top and bottom, with a 1-inch round hole cut in the middle of the *top* piece.
   3. Roll out a ⅜-inch-thick slab of clay, large enough for the six sides of the bottle, plus a ¼-inch strip along one side for the foot. Lay the three pattern pieces on the slab, cut them out with the small knife; then shift the patterns and cut out three more pieces, cutting out the center circular hole on what will be the top of the bottle. Cut out the ¼-inch-wide strip 12 inches in length for the foot.
   4. Allow the six pieces to dry until they can be handled, and they will stand upright without collapsing. Put the bottle together following the directions in Chapter 3. Start with one side piece centered on top of the short side of the base rectangle. Add and attach a wide section. Next, attach the second narrow section. Finally, attach the last wide section. Use slip and thin rolls of clay. The top piece with the cut-out hole is the last one to go into place over the top of the four side sections. Add the ¼-inch-wide strip ¼ inch in from the bottom edges of the bottle for the foot, flattening its bottom so the bottle will be evenly balanced.

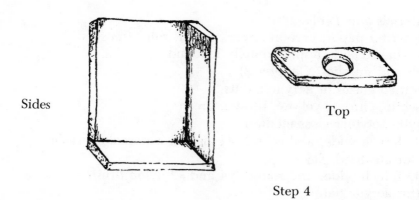

Sides

Top

Step 4

5. Roll out two coils, each one ¼ inch in diameter and 3 inches long for the top loops. Add them, using slip, to the top of the bottle, one on each side between the edge of the hole and the narrow side of the bottle.

Step 5

6. Let the bottle dry until leather hard, then smooth all surfaces with a damp sponge and the wire tool, slightly rounding the top and bottom edges. Let dry thoroughly, then sandpaper all surfaces, if needed, before baking the bottle in the oven.

7. Bake the bottle in the oven, following directions in Chapter 4.

8. After the bottle has been baked and cooled, cover all surfaces plus the two handles with either the white air-dried glaze or white acrylic paint, using the flat ¾-inch-wide brush. Let the coat dry completely before adding the color decorations, otherwise they will spread into the white covering.

9. While the white surfaces are drying, enlarge the rabbit-and-tree pattern on the typewriter paper, following enlarging directions in Chapter 2. Transfer the rabbit-and-tree drawing to the front panel of the bottle. With pencil and ruler measure and draw a ¼-inch-wide border around the outside edges of the front and back panels.

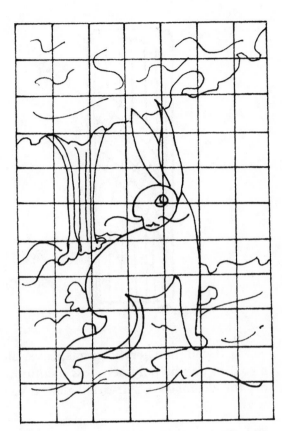

Step 9

Front Design

Enlarge to ½" squares

10. Fill in the rabbit and the front and back borders with a dull ochre color. This is made by mixing a little brown with the chrome yellow air-dried glaze or acrylic paint. Use the #4 round brush. Let the paint dry thoroughly.

11. With the green air-dried glaze or green acrylic paint, fill in freehand the line pattern on each narrow side, using the #2 brush. Fill in the green tree on the front of the bottle using the #4 brush. Set aside for three or four days until thoroughly dry.

12. When the tree is dry, outline the tree with the brown color, adding a few vertical lines on the trunk, and squiggly lines on the foliage and ground using the #2 brush. Also outline the rabbit with the brown color. Let the bottle dry thoroughly.

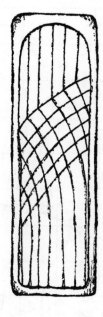

Step 11

Side Design

13. If you used acrylic paints, cover all sides of the bottle with a coat of acrylic polymer gloss medium, and allow the bottle to dry for several days. Air-dried glaze does not need this extra coat.

HARLEQUIN BOWL

In China, toward the end of the 1600s in the K'ang Hsi period of the Ch'ing Dynasty, very thinly-potted, white porcelain bowls were decorated with splashes of green, yellow and brown; a design variously known in English as Harlequin or Spinach-and-Egg. The shape is very elegant and the colors bright and clear.

This bowl is built-up with coils of clay, but you will not be able to make a bowl as thin as the original, as oven-baked clay does not form as strong a "wall" as does high-fired porcelain.

Materials and Tools
lightweight cardboard, pencil, ruler, scissors
oven-baked clay, approximately 1 pound

tools and supplies (Chapter 2)
air-dried glaze or acrylic paint,
    white, green, chrome yellow, brown
acrylic polymer gloss medium
flat, ¾ inch wide, and #4 round watercolor brushes
    (for air-dried glaze)
flat, ¾ inch wide, and #4 round nylon brushes
    (for acrylic paint)

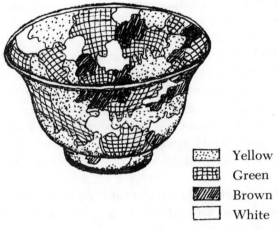

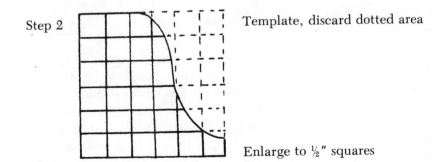

Yellow
Green
Brown
White

Directions
    1. First read the directions in Chapter 3 for making a coil pot.
    2. Enlarge the template pattern onto the cardboard, following the directions in Chapter 2. Cut out the template with the scissors.

Step 2   Template, discard dotted area

Enlarge to ½″ squares

3. Pat out a clay disk, 2 inches in diameter and ½ inch thick; center the disk on a plaster bat or tile.

4. Build up the bowl with a series of coils, ¼ inch in diameter, checking the shape with the template, following the directions in Chapter 3. The final bowl will be 3 inches high and 6 inches in diameter across the top.

5. Set the bowl aside to dry until leather-hard. Cut out the bottom foot, following directions in Chapter 3, Cutting the Foot. Smooth the sides with a damp sponge and the wire tool.

6. Let the bowl dry completely for several days, then go over the whole surface with sandpaper, if necessary.

7. Bake the bowl in the oven, following directions in Chapter 4.

8. After the bowl has been baked and cooled, cover the inside and the outside surfaces with white air-dried glaze or acrylic paint, using the flat brush. Following the glazing or painting directions in Chapter 4. Let the white surface dry completely before adding the other colors. When dry, add the random splashings of yellow, green and brown paint on both the inside and outside surfaces; allow each color to dry before adding the next color with a clean brush.

9. If you have used acrylic paint for the colors, then cover the inside and outside surfaces with acrylic gloss medium as a final finish. The air-dried glaze does not need this additional cover.

10. Set the bowl aside to dry completely.

FLOWER POT: YUAN-MING

For this project, you will recreate an oblong flower pot that is five inches high and was made sometime between 1260 to 1644 A.D. in China, of very high-fired clay known as stoneware. The glaze was a thick, light blue-green, which in the heat of firing created a thin brown line along all the edges of the pot. The Yuan Period founded as a Mongol Dynasty by Kublai Khan, grandson of Genghis Khan, was between the Sung and Ming periods, and many of the clay pieces were still made in the styles and glazes of the earlier Sung potters.

The project pot is the same size as that earlier pot, and in the same color.

Materials and Tools
typewriter paper, pencil, ruler, scissors
oven-baked clay, approximately 1 to 2 pounds
tools and supplies for rolling out clay (Chapter 2)
aid-dried glazes or acrylic paints light blue-green, brown
acrylic polymer gloss medium
flat ¾ inch wide, and round #2 watercolor brushes
    (for air-dried glazes)
flat ¾ inch wide, and round #2 nylon brushes
    (for acrylic paint)

Directions
1. First, read the directions in Chapter 3 for making a Box Shape, as this container is essentially a box without a covered top.
2. Enlarge the patterns for the sides and bottom, and the bottom strips on the typewriter paper (see Chapter 2, Enlarging, Reducing and Transferring Designs). Cut them out with the scissors.
3. Roll out a ½-inch-thick slab (or two slabs) large enough for the four sides, bottom, and four bottom strips. Lay the patterns over the clay and cut out the pieces, then carefully remove all the

Steps 2 and 3

Enlarge to ½″ squares

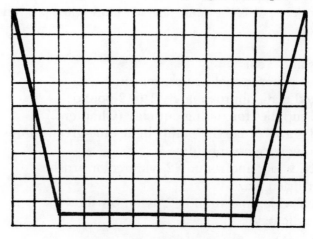

Front and Back

Sides

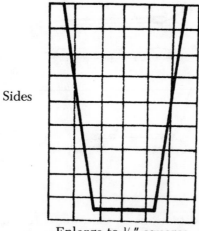

Enlarge to ½″ squares

Bottom Strips

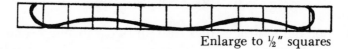

Enlarge to ½″ squares

Steps 2 and 3

Bottom

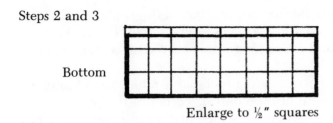

Enlarge to ½″ squares

excess clay scraps. Allow the pieces to dry undisturbed until they can be lifted up without bending over, but do not let them stay until leather-hard.

4. Put the bottom and sides together with slip and rolls of clay that are ⅛ inch in diameter, following directions in Chapter 3. The long sides extend over the short sides (see drawing). Add an extra roll of clay, ¼ inch in diameter to each inside corner, squaring off the outer sides (see drawing).

Step 4

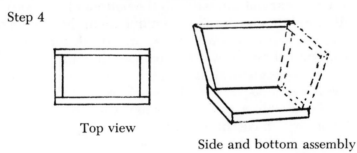

Top view

Side and bottom assembly

5. For the top edge, roll or pat out four, ¼-inch-thick strips, ¾ inch wide; two of the strips should be 6 inches long, and two, 3 inches long. With slip and ⅛-inch-diameter rolls of clay, add the strips along the top edge of the pot on the outer ¼ inch of the ½-inch-thick walls of the pot (see drawing).

Step 5

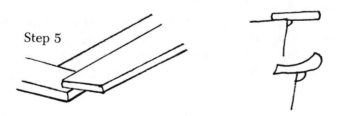

6. To decorate this top edging draw a finger along the top of the clay to make a shallow, concave indentation, lifting the outer edge up slightly and rounding it. Mark curved nicks at each corner (see drawing).

7. With the wire modeling tool, carve a half-round indentation down the length of each outside corner of the pot.

8. Form four coils of clay, ½ inch in diameter and 1 inch long to make the four feet at the bottom of the pot. Squeeze and mold the coils into shape following the drawing. Add the feet to the bottom of each corner with slip, cutting out a little triangle of clay on the top of each foot so the corner will fit into place.

 Step 8

9. Add the four bottom strips to the bottom of the pot with slip and thin rolls of clay, each one ending up in the middle of a foot. Curve the strips outward as they are added, forming each end into a rounded bump over the foot (see drawing).

10. Set the pot aside until it is leather-hard, then go over all surfaces with a damp sponge and wire modeling tool to smooth them. Set aside for three or four days to dry thoroughly.

11. When dry, bake in the oven following directions in Chapter 4.

12. When the pot has cooled, cover all surfaces with the light blue-green glaze or acrylic paint. Let dry. Add a narrow brown line with the #2 brush, along all the edges to match the original pot. Let dry. If you have used acrylic paint, then cover all surfaces with the gloss medium and let it dry thoroughly. Air-dried glaze will not need a final clear coat.

Note: If you are making this pot of regular clay and firing it in a kiln, with kiln-fired glaze, then it can be used as a plant container. In this case, you will have to make a round hole ½ inch in diameter in the middle of the bottom to act as a water drainer for the soil.

FOOD JAR: CHINESE WARRING STATES

The original unglazed food jar was made long ago in western China sometime during the last 250 years of the Chou (Zhou) Dynasty, which had lasted for nine centuries. In the period from 475 to 221 B.C. the territory broke up into semi-independent states which were constantly involved in border disputes, and so came to be known as the Warring States.

This type of jar has been found in tombs, and was made to hold food for use in the afterlife. A coarsely woven piece of cloth was pressed against the still moist surface of the clay, then removed, leaving the woven pattern as a surface decoration.

Your jar will be 6 inches high and 8 inches across at the widest point. The original Chinese jar was 8 inches high and 10 inches across. Unlike the original, you will be covering the inside and outside surfaces with a "glaze" of acrylic polymer matte medium, as oven-baked clay needs a hard covering so the surface will not "dust off."

Materials and Tools
lightweight cardboard, pencil, ruler, scissors
oven-baked clay, approximately 1 pound
tools and other supplies (Chapter 2)
cheesecloth, 15 × 20 inches
acrylic polymer matte medium
flat, ¾ inch wide nylon brush

Directions

    1. First read the directions in Chapter 3 for forming Coil Pots.

    2. Enlarge the template pattern onto the cardboard; cut out the pattern with the scissors. Follow the directions in Chapter 2 for enlarging a pattern.

Template, discard dotted area

Step 2

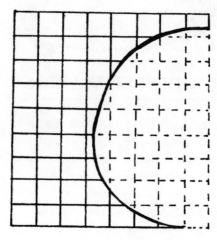

Enlarge to ¾" squares

    3. Pat out a clay disk, 4 inches in diameter and ½ inch thick and center it on a plaster bat or tile.

    4. Build up the jar with coils ½ inch in diameter, attaching the first coil at the *side* of the clay disk, since the bottom of the jar is flat and has no foot. As you add coils, check the shape with the template. The top opening is 2 inches in diameter. Smooth the surface with the sponge.

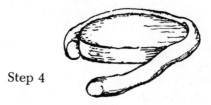

Step 4

5. Make three cones, 1 inch high and ⅝ inch in diameter at the top; see illustration for shape. Turn the jar upside down, and attach the three cones to the bottom with slip and thin rolls of clay. The cones are placed at equal distances from each other in a triangle, approximately around the edges of the 4-inch disk. Let the cones harden a bit, then turn the jar right side up.

Step 5

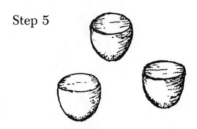

6. While the jar's surface is moist (or if it has started to dry, moisten it with a damp sponge), drape the cheesecloth around the jar, stretching it and pressing it against the surface. Remove the cloth carefully so as to leave the imprint on the clay.

7. Pat out a ¼-inch-thick strip, 9 inches long and ¾ inch wide for the handle. Curve it into shape, following the drawing, then allow it to stiffen enough to hold the shape. Attach the handle to the jar with slip. Be very careful not to smear the surface pattern.

8. Set the jar aside for three or four days to dry completely before baking.

9. Bake the jar in the oven following the directions given in Chapter 4 (Baking Clay).

10. When the pot has been baked and cooled, cover the inside and outside of the pot, and the handle and feet with the clear, acrylic polymer matte medium using the flat ¾-inch-wide brush (see Chapter 4 for directions). Let dry thoroughly.

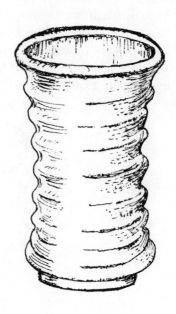

SUNG BRUSH HOLDER

The potters in the Sung period in China (960–1279 A.D.) produced many different forms of vases, bowls, and ceremonial urns, all in a glaze that ranged in color from a pale greenish-blue called celadon to a light to medium brownish olive-green.

This brush holder is 5 inches high and approximately 2¼ inches wide with ridged sides and a 3¼-inch-inch flared top. You will not need a template for this pot as its shape is simple.

Materials and Tools
oven-baked clay, approximately 1 pound
tools and supplies for coil pots (Chapter 2)
air-dried glazes, or acrylic paints, olive green, brown
acrylic polymer gloss medium
flat watercolor brush, ¾ inch wide
   (for air-dried glazes)
flat nylon brush, ¾ inch wide
   (for acrylic paint and medium)

Directions

1. First read the directions for making Coil Pots in Chapter 3.

2. Pat out a 2 × ½-inch clay disk as the base of the pot, and place it on a plaster bat or tile.

3. Form a clay coil ¾ inch in diameter and long enough to fit around the edge of the clay disk. Smear clay slip around the top edge of the disk, and place the coil in position. The coil will be wider than the disk, 2⅝ inches in diameter. Make a good bond between disk and coil on both the inside and outside, curving the outer edge to follow the outline of the drawing.

Step 4

Step 3

4. Build up the pot with six coils, ¾ inch in diameter, smoothing the inside but keeping an outside pattern of coil shapes. This section is 2¼ inches in diameter.

5. The last two coils will form the flared top; the first is a little smoother than the previous coils, the second and top coil is smoothed out and flared to form a top 3¼ inches in diameter.

6. When the pot is leather-hard, smooth the outside and inside surfaces with the wire tool and damp sponge. Turn the pot upside down and cut out the foot (see Chapter 3, Cutting the Foot). Set the pot aside for several days to dry thoroughly.

7. Bake the pot in the oven, following the directions given in Chapter 4 (Baking Clay).

8. When the pot has been baked and cooled, add the color to all surfaces inside and out. You may choose either air-dried glaze or acrylic paint. See Chapter 4 (Coloring and Glazing the Clay Pot) for directions on mixing the color and applying the colored coat. If using acrylic paint, cover it with the gloss medium when dry. Set the pot aside until the glaze or acrylic covering is thoroughly dry.

Eastern Mediterranean

BYZANTINE PLATE

The Byzantine Empire was at its height from 476 to 1453 A.D. It stretched around the Mediterranean Sea from Corsica and Carthage in the west to beyond the Black Sea in the east. Today, in Italy, you can see frescoes and bas-relief carvings in churches that are Byzantine, as well as mosaic decorations. This plate with its geometric design and simple colors is on display in the ceramic museum in Faenza in northern Italy.

Materials and Tools
typewriter paper, carbon paper, pencil,
    ruler, scissors, compass
oven-baked clay, approximately 1 pound
tools and other supplies (Chapter 2)

60

flat dish for a mold, approximately 8 inches in diameter
air-dried glaze or acrylic paint, white, brown
acrylic polymer gloss medium
flat ¾ inch wide, and round #4 and #2 watercolor brushes
(for air-dried glaze)
flat ¾ inch wide, and round #4 and #2 nylon brushes
(for acrylic paint)

Directions
1. First read the directions in Chapter 3 (Bowls and Plates) for making a slab bowl.

Step 5   Pattern

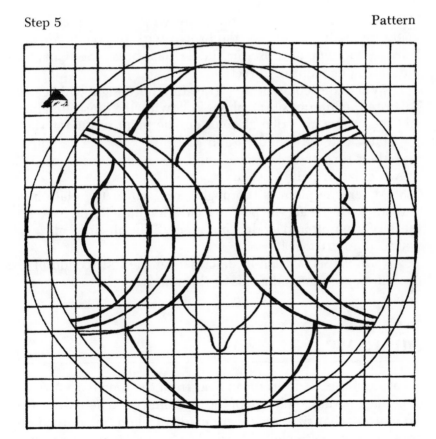

Enlarge to ½" squares

2. Prepare the mold; drape the slab of clay over the bottom; press it lightly into place and trim the edges. Curve a coil of clay into a circle at the center as a foot. Allow the clay to partially stiffen, then remove it from the mold.

3. Once the plate has been removed from the mold, turn it right side up to continue drying until leather-hard. When the clay is leather-hard, smooth the interior and exterior with a damp sponge and the wire tool (see Variation).

4. Dry the plate thoroughly for several days and then bake it in the oven following directions in Chapter 4 (Baking Clay).

5. While the plate is cooling, enlarge the pattern for the interior design on the typewriter paper; see Chapter 2 for directions on enlarging a design.

6. Cover the interior of the plate with a deep cream color made by mixing a little of the brown with the white air-dried glaze or acrylic paint; use the flat ¾-inch brush. See Chapter 4 for glazing or painting directions.

7. When the color is dry, transfer the design with carbon paper to the interior of the plate. Following the illustrated plate, add the brown air-dried glaze or acrylic paint to the interior of the plate. Use the round #4 and #2 brushes for the design. Let dry, then turn the plate over, and cover the outside with the brown glaze or paint. Let dry.

8. When the paint is thoroughly dry, cover the plate inside and out with the acrylic polymer gloss medium if you have used the acrylic paint, and let dry thoroughly. The air-dried glaze will not need an extra coat.

Variation: See *Variation* described in the last section of this book in Southwest-Indian Bowl (Mimbres).

OIL LAMP

All around the Mediterranean Sea, from the fourth century B.C. or perhaps earlier, oil lamps of the type illustrated here were used. No matter what size, they were made of plain, unadorned tan, gray, or terra-cotta clay. There was always a bowl-like opening to hold the oil, a small hole at one side to hold the wick upright as it burned (the rest of the wick coiled in the bowl of oil), and a carrying handle). The bottom was flat so it could be put down on any surface. These were standard household objects, often broken, easily replaced, and so not many have survived the centuries.

This one is very small, with a bowl only 3 inches wide and 1 to 1½ inches deep, and the whole lamp is just less than 5 inches long. It is formed as a "pinch pot." *Note:* This lamp is not for actual use if made with oven-baked clay, because oil will cause the clay to disintegrate. It makes a fine decorative object, though, of real historical interest.

Materials and Tools
typewriter paper, pencil, ruler, scissors
oven-baked clay, approximately 1 pound
tools and other supplies (Chapter 2)
acrylic polymer matte medium
flat, ¾ inch wide nylon brush

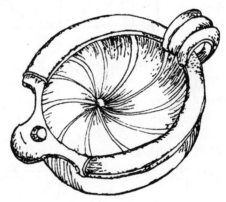

Directions
1. First read the directions in Chapter 3 for making a pinch pot.
2. Pinch out a flat-bottomed shallow, round bowl, 3 inches in diameter with curving sides. The pot should be 1 to 1½ inches deep in the center, and the wall of the bowl is ⅜ inch thick. While the clay is still soft, draw 11 to 12 swirling lines which end at a small indentation in the center of the bowl, using the point of a pencil. Smooth the edges of the lines.

3. Pat out a strip of clay ¼ inch thick, ½ inch wide, and 11 inches long. Next, with slip, add thin rolls of clay no more than ⅛ inch in diameter, against the inside and outside of the bowl's top edge. Smear the tops of the rolls and the bowl's top edge with slip; lay the ½-inch-wide strip of clay on top of them, centering it on the rim of the bowl so it extends over the inside and outside of the bowl's edge. As you curve the strip around the bowl, you will have to nip out little triangles of clay to make a flat, smooth top. With the plastic tool, smooth the rolls of clay up against the strip and against the bowl wall to form a firm, supporting bond.

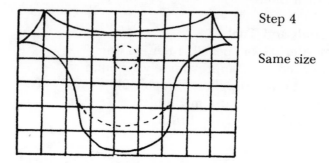

Step 4

Same size

4. Transfer the lip pattern to the typewriter paper by the grid method, and cut out with scissors (see Chapter 2 for making a pattern). Pat out a 1½ × 2¼-inch slab of clay, ¼ inch thick. Lay the paper pattern over the clay and cut out with a pointed knife. Let stiffen a bit. With slip, add the clay lip on top of the clay rim; support it with a wedge of clay that is smoothed down onto the side of the bowl (see drawings for both these processes).

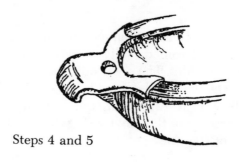

Steps 4 and 5

5. Centered on the lip, make a hole from the rim, angled down to the inside of the bowl. Use a pencil and roll it around to widen the hole to ¼ inch in diameter (see drawing).

6. For the handle, roll out three coils of clay ¼ inch in diameter and 4½ inches long. Anchor each one with slip, side by side, to the ½-inch rim opposite the lip. Hold them together with slip and curve them upward and outward, smoothing their ends into the side of the bowl halfway to the bottom.

7. Set the oil lamp aside until leather-hard, then smooth with a damp sponge and the wire modeling tool. Check the bottom to make sure it is flat. Let dry completely.

8. When the oil lamp is thoroughly dry, bake it in the oven. (See Chapter 4 for directions.)

9. When cool, cover all the surfaces with acrylic polymer matte medium, using the flat ¾-inch-wide brush (see Chapter 4 for directions). Allow the medium to dry for several days.

ROOSTER PLATE: ANATOLIA

Anatolia is the ancient name for the land east of the Aegean Sea, reaching as far as the Black Sea and later known as Asia Minor. Some of this area is now part of Turkey. In the ceramic museum in Faenza, Italy, there is an undated plate from this region. It is cream-colored with a center drawing of a lively, squawking, rust-colored rooster; around the edge are brown, curved lines.

This project plate is much smaller than the original, but the proportions of the design remain the same.

Materials and Tools
typewriter paper, carbon paper, pencil, ruler, scissors, compass
oven-baked clay, approximately 1 pound
tools and supplies (Chapter 2)
flat dish for a mold approximately 8 inches in diameter, with a 1½-inch broad rim
air-dried glaze or acrylic paint, white, brown, rust
acrylic polymer gloss medium
flat ¾ inch wide, and round #4 and #2 watercolor brushes (for air-dried glaze)
flat ¾ inch wide, and round #4 and #2 nylon brushes (for acrylic paint)

Directions
1. First read the directions in Chapter 3 (Bowls and Plates) for making a slab plate.
2. Prepare the dish mold as described in Chapter 3 and drape the slab of clay over the bottom of the flat dish which you have previously covered with plastic wrap. Press the clay slab slightly into place over the bottom surface of the dish mold and trim the edges. Curve a coil of clay into a circle 2½ inches in diameter. Place the clay circle in the center of the slab to form a foot on what will be the bottom of your plate. Allow the clay to partially stiffen, then remove from the mold.
3. Turn the newly made plate right side up. With your fingers held together, lightly press downward all over the center of the plate, forming a 6½-inch-diameter circle into a shallow bowl. The 1½-inch margin remains flat. Let the clay dry until leather hard, then smooth the inside and outside of the plate with a damp sponge and wire tool (for possible variation see below).

4. Dry the plate thoroughly for several days, then bake in the oven following the directions in Chapter 4.

5. While the plate is cooling, copy the design for the interior on typewriter paper. Follow directions in Chapter 2 for copying a same-size drawing.

Step 5   Same size

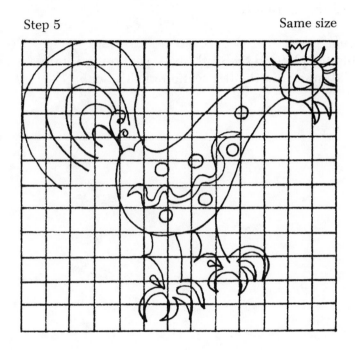

6. Reread the directions in Chapter 4 for glazing or painting the clay. For the base cream color mix a little of the brown color with the white air-dried glaze or acrylic paint. Cover the inside of the plate with this cream color using the flat ¾-inch brush, and let dry. Turn the plate over, and cover the back with the cream color glaze or paint, and let dry.

7. When the cream-colored coat is dry, transfer the rooster design to the inside center of the plate, using carbon paper. Outline the rooster with the rust air-dried glaze or acrylic paint using the #4 and #2 brushes.

8. Add the brown, curved lines around the edge of the plate following the design in the illustration. Set the plate aside for several days to dry thoroughly.

9. If you have used acrylic paints, cover the outside and the inside of the plate with a coat of acrylic polymer gloss medium, and allow the plate to dry for several days. Air-dried glaze does not need this extra coat.

Variation
To hang the plate on the wall, see *Variation* in Southwest-Indian Bowl (Mimbres) in the last section of this book.

Egypt

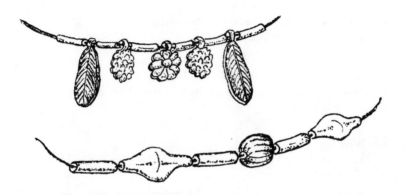

BEADS AND PENDANTS

During many centuries, from 2000 to 1350 B.C., Egyptian neck-laces were made of both semiprecious stones, and highly glazed and colored pottery. Both the beads and pendants were made in many shapes—narrow cylinders, plain round or with a melon design, rounded diamonds, oval seed shapes. The pendants which hung between beads were colorful leaf, fruit and flower shapes, as well as scarabs colored blue and gray-green.

In this project you will choose the size of the beads and pendants, designing the necklace to suit your taste. You become an Egyptian craftsperson, using the necklace forms of ancient times as you put together jewelry of your own design. See the detailed drawings of several bead and pendant forms you can combine into a necklace. You can also add the scarab design (see scarab project in this section) as either a large center pendant, or make several small scarabs to hang between the other small pendants.

Materials and Tools
ruler
oven-baked clay—several tablespoons
thin nail, skewer or round toothpicks
thin wire, 24 inches or longer
2 jars, approximately 4 inches high
air-dried glaze or acrylic paint, white, rust, yellow, green,
    bright blue
acrylic polymer gloss medium
round #4 and #2 watercolor brushes
    (for air-dried glaze)
round #4 and #2 nylon brushes
    (for acrylic paint and medium)
nylon bead cord, or button and carpet thread
ring catch and loop

Directions
   1. First, read the directions in Chapter 3 (Coil Pots) on form-ing clay coils.
   2. To make round beads of equal size, roll a clay coil ¼ inch in diameter, or whatever thickness you want your beads to be. Measure off equal distances along the coil, and cut off each sec-tion with a small knife. Roll these pieces into round beads between the palms of your hands.
   3. Make a hole through the center of each bead with a small nail, skewer, or round toothpick, large enough to hold the thread you will string the beads on, allowing for the shrinkage of clay. Some of the beads can be marked with lines from hole to hole (melon pattern), or around the circumference of the bead—or just left plain.
   4. Wrap one end of the wire around the top groove of an empty jelly or similar jar and fasten securely. String the beads on the wire to dry, spacing them so they do not touch. Fasten the other end of the wire around the top groove of the second jar; stretch the bead-laden wire between the two jars. Dry beads thoroughly before baking.
   5. To make cylinder beads, either even widths or ovals, cut equal size pieces of clay from a coil. Roll these pieces into small

coils ¼ inch in diameter and ½ to ¾ inches long. Make a hole through the center of each bead, and, with a small knife make a straight, vertical cut at each end. String the cylinders on wire to dry.

    6. For the rounded diamond shapes, pinch and squeeze the clay coil sections into the desired shape; make a center hole; dry the beads by stringing them on the wire.

Beads   Pendants

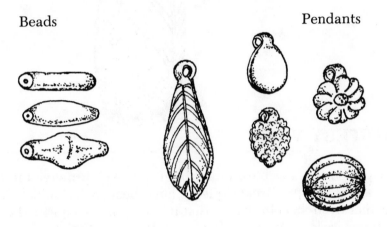

    7. Form the pendants by patting out the clay, cutting and pinching it into pendant shapes, marking the surface designs with a thin nail, skewer, or toothpicks. Dry on a flat surface before baking.

    8. When all the beads and pendants are dry, bake them in the oven following directions in Chapter 4.

    9. After the beads and pendants have cooled, mix and apply the glazes or acrylic paints, following the directions in Chapter 4.

    10. Wait until the beads and pendants are thoroughly dry, then string them on the nylon bead cord or the heavy button and carpet thread, adding a ring catch and loop at each end to fasten the necklace. Or make a long necklace which will go over your head—then you will not need a ring catch, just tie a strong knot with the ends of your stringing cord or thread.

    11. Hang the pendants by separate loops of thread or cord, tied between the beads. See drawing.

POTTERY VASE

Ancient pottery has been found in graves, well preserved in the dry air of Egypt. Broken pieces have been painstakingly put together by archaeologists, so that in museums we can see the art of those early potters. This vase is from an Egyptian period known as Pre-Dynasty, or roughly before 3200 B.C. when the "Dynastic Egyptians" came down from the north. The original of this vase is in the British Museum collection, along with many other pottery vases from that period, all with different designs.

The project vase is six inches tall, with a rust-red glaze decorated with slightly raised white lines, the inside painted white.

Materials and Tools
lightweight cardboard, pencil, ruler, scissors
oven-dried clay, approximately 1 pound
tools and supplies (Chapter 2)
air-dried glaze or acrylic paint, rust-red, white
acrylic polymer gloss medium
flat ¾ inch wide, and #2 round watercolor brushes
  (for air-dried glazes)
flat ¾ inch wide, and #2 round nylon brushes
  (for acrylic paint and medium)

Directions

    1. First, read the directions in Chapter 3 for making a coil pot.

    2. Enlarge the template pattern onto the lightweight cardboard, following directions in Chapter 2. Cut out the template with scissors.

Template, discard dotted area

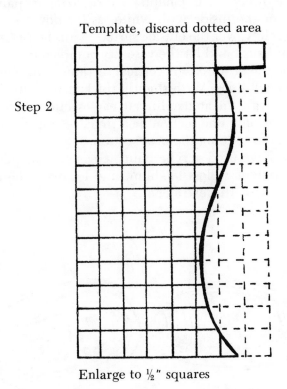

Step 2

Enlarge to ½" squares

    3. Pat out a clay disk 1¾ inches in diameter, and ½ inch thick; center the disk on a plaster bat or tile.

    4. Starting on the outside, top edge of the disk, build up the vase with coils that are ⅜ inch in diameter, checking the shape with the template, and following the directions in Chapter 3. The final jar will be 6 inches high, 2¼ to 2½ inches in diameter at the widest part, and 1¼ inches in diameter at the top.

    5. Let the vase dry to leather hard, then turn it over and cut a ¼-inch-deep foot on the bottom, following directions in Chapter 3.

6. Smooth all surfaces with a damp sponge and the wire modeling tool. Let the jar dry thoroughly for several days before baking.

7. Bake the jar in the oven, following directions in Chapter 4.

8. After the jar has been baked and cooled, add color, following the directions in Chapter 4 for glazing or painting the surfaces. Color the inside with white, as far down as your flat brush will reach. Cover the outside surface with the rust-red color, using the flat brush and let the vase dry completely.

9. Divide the jar into four vertical sections, and lightly mark these with pencil lines. With slightly thickened white color and the #2 brush, draw the angled lines in each section, following the drawing. Paint only one section at a time, letting the color dry thoroughly, before doing the next section.

10. If you have used acrylic paint, cover the outside surface with acrylic polymer gloss medium, and let dry. The air-dried glaze will not need this extra coat.

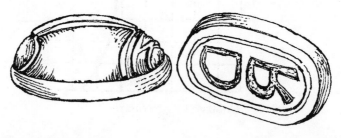

SCARAB SEAL

In ancient Egypt, a beetle was the symbol of eternal life, and so beetle-like designs called scarabs were worn as charms to bring good fortune and chase away misfortune. They were made of baked and glazed clay, or carved from semiprecious stones. Often the owner's sign or name was carved on the flat bottom, and this was used to stamp documents, official papers, or packages of goods, as an identifying mark.

This scarab design, with your initials carved on the flat bottom *in reverse* (so they will be in the right direction when stamped on paper), is made of clay colored a light gray-green. Use an ink pad with your choice of color to transfer the design to paper.

The same scarab design can be turned into a pendant to be worn on a cord, or into smaller sizes which can form a necklace with the addition of round or oval beads glazed in the same gray-green or dark blue, or both colors as a present you can make for mother.

Materials and Tools
typewriter paper, pencil, ruler, scissors
clear plastic wrap, 8 × 12 inches
sticky cellophane tape
oven-baked clay, approximately 2 to 3 tablespoons
tools and other supplies (Chapter 2)
thin nail, skewer, or round toothpicks
acrylic paint, white and light blue-green
acrylic polymer gloss medium
round #4 nylon brush

Directions
1. Copy the pattern on the typewriter paper, using the grid method, following the directions in Chapter 2. Cover the paper with clear plastic wrap, and hold in place with sticky tape, so that the clay will not smear the pencil pattern.

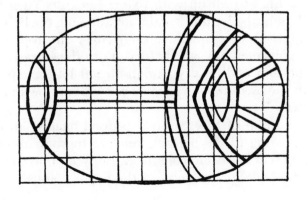

Step 1

Same size

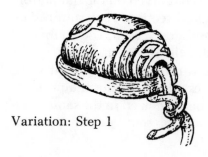

Variation: Step 1

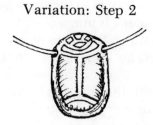

Variation: Step 2

2. Starting with one tablespoon of clay, smooth it over the pattern, building up a flat oval, ¼ inch thick, with straight sides around the outer edge. Then add more clay to make a long, gently-rounded shape that is about 1½ inches high in the center.

3. Follow the drawing in marking the top and sides of the scarab, using a thin nail, skewer, or round toothpick.

4. Let the scarab dry until almost leather hard. Remove it from the paper, turn it over, and deeply carve your initials, *reversed*, on the back, adding an outline near the outer edge. Smooth all surfaces with a damp sponge, making sure that there are no crumbles of clay from the carved lines.

5. Let the clay dry thoroughly for several days, then bake in the oven following directions in Chapter 4.

6. See coloring directions in Chapter 4. Mix the acrylic paint, gradually adding white paint to the blue-green paint to lighten and soften the color. Paint the top and sides, but be careful not to allow the carved lines to fill up with paint. Let dry. Turn the scarab over and paint the bottom, again not allowing the lines to fill up with paint. Dry completely, then cover the top with acrylic polymer gloss medium, and let dry. Turn the scarab over and cover the bottom and let dry. Again *do not* let the carved lines fill up with the medium—if you do, you will not be able to print the initials.

7. When the bottom of the scarab is pressed against an ink pad, the ink will cling to the bottom, but not to your initials. Your seal printing will be a solid color oval, but your initials and the border will be white or the color of the paper you use.

Variations

1. If you are going to use the scarab as a pendant, make a small hole at the head of the scarab so it can be hung on a cord. The hole must be a little larger than the cord to allow for clay shrinkage.

2. If you are making a necklace, then the scarabs should be ¾ to 1 inch long, and you can pinch and mold them to the proper shape by looking at the drawing. Add a hole at the head with a toothpick, so the scarabs can be strung on nylon bead thread. Make as many scarabs as you will need for your design. See page 70 for a description of bead making.

England

CRUSADER DESIGN TILE

This tile is copied from a fourteenth-century tile, one of several tiles still part of the floor of Romsey Abbey in Romsey, a small town about ten miles from Winchester, England. The type is typical of various Crusader designs.

The technique is known as *Encaustic*—a set-in design. First a raised design was carved into a block of wood, and the wood block design was pressed into soft, earth-colored clay slabs. The slabs were then cut into shapes—square, oblong, triangular, or round; the shallow sunken design was then carefully filled with white clay. After the tiles had been fired, the surface was covered with a clear lead glaze.

Tiles of this type are very rare, as they were usually used to cover church floors. Walked on every day and, being low-fired, they soon crumbled or cracked—and so through the years they were replaced with sturdier, plain tiles.

Encaustic technique cannot be used for oven-baked clay, as no white clay exists for very low temperatures. Instead, in this project, the design is painted on the surface with white glaze or acrylic paint, then covered with clear air-dried glaze or acrylic polymer matte medium. If you are firing the tiles in a regular kiln with regular clay, then you can experiment with this technique, cutting the design in a linoleum block, but reversing the drawing.

Materials and Tools
typewriter paper, pencil, ruler, scissors, carbon paper
oven-baked clay—approximately 1 pound
tools and other supplies (Chapter 2)
air-dried glaze or acrylic paint, white, clear glaze
acrylic polymer matte medium
flat, ¾ inch wide, and #4 and #2 round watercolor brushes
    (for air-dried glazes)
flat, ¾ inch wide, and #4 and #2 round nylon brushes
    (for acrylic paint and medium)

Directions
1. First, read the directions in Chapter 3 for rolling out clay slabs.
2. Roll out sufficient clay for a 5 × 5 inch tile, ½ inch thick. Measure and cut out the tile with the point of a small knife. Carefully remove the excess clay from around the edges of the tile. Let the tile dry without disturbing it until the clay is stiff enough to allow the tile to be lifted up without spoiling its shape.
3. Cut out the bottom foot with the wire modeling tool (see Chapter 3, Cutting a Foot).
4. Let the clay dry until leather hard, then smooth all surfaces with a damp sponge.
5. After several days, when the tile is completely dry, bake it in the oven, following directions for baking in Chapter 4.
6. While the tile is baking, enlarge the design on the typewriter

Enlarge to ½" squares

paper by the grid method following directions in Chapter 2 (Enlarging, Reducing, and Transferring Designs).

7. When the tile has been baked and cooled, transfer the design to the tile with carbon paper. Fill in the design with either white air-dried glaze, or white acrylic paint, using the #4 and #2 brushes and following directions in Chapter 4. Let dry until hard.

8. Cover all surfaces of the tile with either clear air-dried glaze, or acrylic polymer matte glaze, depending on which material you used in Step 7. Use the flat ¾-inch-wide brush. Let dry until hard.

DEVON COTTAGE

Tiny copies of English cottages are classic designs that have been made by generations of potters. Styles vary from region to region of England, reflecting the type of country or town buildings found in each area. Cottages made in the Victorian period and earlier, were made with a hole down the length of the chimney so that the incense burned inside to freshen the air of a room, would form a realistic plume of smoke. Other cottages had a slit

in the roof and were used as "penny" banks. And then there are
cottages that have no function at all—they are just made to be
looked at.

This thatched, Devon cottage, a copy of one made by John
Putnam of England for his collection of Heritage Houses, is formed
from clay slabs like a box, with a separate base. The painted,
oven-baked clay should not be used to burn incense in, but it
makes a fine bank for coins dropped through a slit in the roof. Its
shape is rectangular, and is about 2 × 3¼ inches and 3½ inches
high at the peak of the roof.

Materials and Tools
typewriter paper, ruler, pencil, scissors, carbon paper
oven-baked clay, approximately 1 pound
tools and supplies (Chapter 2)
air-dried glazes or acrylic paints, white, tan, black,
    rust, blue, green
acrylic polymer gloss medium
flat, ¾ inch wide, and round #4 and #2 watercolor brushes
    (for air-dried glaze)
flat, ¾ inch wide, and round #4 and #2 nylon brushes
    (for acrylic paint)

Step 2   Enlarge to ½″ squares

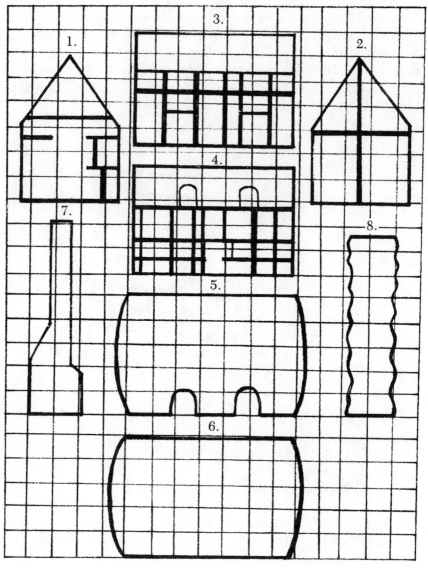

1. Left side   2. Right side   3. Back   4. Front   5. Roof front
6.   Roof back   7. Chimney   8.   Roof overlap

Directions

1. First read the directions in Chapter 3 for making a slab Box Shape.

2. Enlarge the patterns for the cottage on the typewriter paper and cut out the separate pieces with the scissors. Cut away the window and door areas. See Chapter 2, for enlarging the pattern.

3. Roll out a ¼-inch-thick slab which is large enough for the sections. Lay the sides, and the two large roof patterns, over the top surface of the slab, and cut out the pieces. Measure and cut out a 3 × 4¼-inch slab as a base for the cottage. Thin out the remaining slab to ⅛ inch thick, and cut out the chimney section as well as the narrow overlapping section of the roof.

4. When the clay sections are stiff enough to handle, cut and scrape out shallow 1/16-inch-deep areas of the windows and door. Put the four sections together following directions in Chapter 3; the front and back pieces overlapping the sides (a & b). Add the chimney in the center of the left hand side of the cottage (c). Add extra, thin slabs to the top of the chimney to form the upper square above the roof (see diagram).

5. Add the two large roof sections, joining them to the house sections (overlapping the front and back sections), cutting out the left sides at the peak around the chimney. Curve the thin, overlapping section of the roof over the peak-joining of the two roof sections, cutting away the section around the chimney.

6. Put the cottage in the center of the separate base slab. build up a ¼-inch-high ridge of clay coils on top of the exposed margin of the base slab. Smooth the surface of the ridge, curving the front down to the height of the slab. Form hollows and bumps on the surface with your fingers to give the effect of uneven ground. Remove the cottage, and let both the cottage and base dry to leather hard.

7. When the clay is leather hard, scratch in the thatch design on the roof with the tines of a table fork. Cut a 1 × 3/16-inch slit in the roof at the back if you are going to use the cottage as a penny bank. Smooth the sides of the cottage with a damp sponge and wire tool. Set cottage aside for three or four days to dry thoroughly. Repeat the smoothing on the base slab, then set it aside to dry.

8. When the cottage and base are completely dry, bake them in the oven, following the directions in Chapter 4.

Step 4

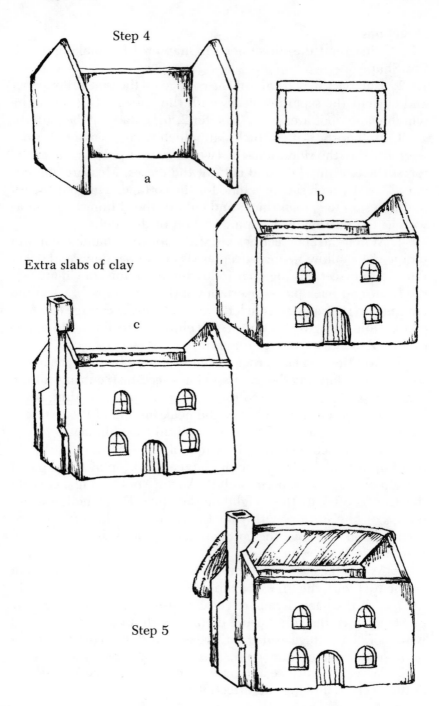

a

b

Extra slabs of clay

c

Step 5

9. After the cottage and separate base have been baked and cooled, cover the cottage outside and inside (except the chimney) with either air-dried white glaze or white acrylic paint. Cover the top and bottom surfaces of the base with either air-dried white glaze or white acrylic paint. Set both pieces aside to dry thoroughly before adding the other colors. The flat brush is best for this painting. Follow glazing or painting directions in Chapter 4.

10. Cover the thatched roof with the light tan color using the ¾-inch flat brush—be very careful and do not dribble any paint on the white sides of the house. With the #4 brush, cover the chimney with the rust color. Clean the brush, and color the curved ridge around the edge of the base with the green. Let all the colors dry. When the roof and chimney are dry, then add the light blue color to the windows, lightly scratching a cross mark on each window with the point of a skewer or nail so a white line shows through the blue. Repeat this process with the blue color on the door, scratching vertical lines through to the white color below. Let dry.

11. With the small #2 brush draw the narrow black lines on the four sides of the house, following the lines on the patterns. You can either draw these freehand, or transfer the lines with carbon paper onto the white sides of the cottage. Set aside to dry.

12. If you have used acrylic paint to cover and decorate the cottage and the separate base, then add a final coat of acrylic polymer gloss medium inside and outside of the cottage, and on the top and bottom of the base. Set aside to thoroughly dry before using.

TUDOR ROSE MUG

This is a modern, straight-sided mug based on an old pewter mug design. It is decorated with two applied, low-relief designs of a Tudor rose in a contrasting color. The professional potter's phrase for this type of decoration is "sprigged on," which means anything attached to a greenware (unbaked) pot. A Tudor rose doesn't look much like a modern rose, because it is based on the simple wild roses of 500 years ago.

Use the mug to hold pencils or a dried flower arrangement. You can't use it to hold liquids because it will dissolve. You can add your name or any other design to this basic mug if you like. The possibilities are endless.

Materials and Tools
typewriter paper, pencil, ruler, scissors
oven-baked clay, approximately 1 pound
straight-sided bottle or can as a mold (see Step 2)
tools and other supplies (Chapter 2)
air-dried glaze or acrylic paint, white, brown, blue
acrylic polymer matte medium
flat watercolor brush, ¾ inch wide (for air-dried glaze)
flat nylon brush, ¾ inch wide (for acrylic paint and medium)

Directions

1. First read the directions in Chapter 3 for forming slab pots.

2. The straight-sided bottle or can to be used as a mold should be about 4½ inches high and a minimum of 3½ inches in diameter. If the mold is higher, you can still just roll out a 4½-inch-wide slab. The length of the slab has to be enough to equal the circumference of the mold, plus one inch for the two handle strips, plus the size of the bottom disk of the mug (which is approxi-

mately 3¾ inches), in other words, at least 8¼ inches long. The slab is ¼-inch thick. Measure the circumference of the mold (the distance around the outside of the bottle or can) with a length of string and add 1 inch.

3. Roll out the slab, measure and cut out the length for the mug, and the two ½-inch strips for the handle. The bottom disk will be cut out later.

4. When the slab is stiff enough to lift up, but not so stiff that it cannot be curved around the mold, remove it from the plastic work surface. Wrap the slab around the plastic-covered mold; cut away any excess clay at the joining; brush the ends with slip, smoothing them together. Let the clay dry only until it will stand alone. Set the clay-covered mold on a sheet of typewriter paper and draw around the circumference, making the pattern for the bottom disk of the mug. Cut out the pattern, lay it over the remaining slab of clay, and cut out the disk.

5. Remove the cylinder of clay from the mold. Scratch around the top edge of the disk and smear the scratch marks with clay slip. Place the cylinder on top of the disk and seal the edges outside and inside.

6. Following the drawing, curve the bottom and the top of the mug into outward flaring edges. You can add two incised lines around the bottom of the mug. Cut an angled bevel (sloping edge) at the bottom of the mug.

7. Drag the tines of a table fork down one side of each of the two clay handle pieces, to form parallel lines. Curve the two pieces of the handle across each other and attach them to the side of the mug, top and bottom with slip, smoothing the joining with the plastic tool and fingers. Follow the drawing for placement.

Step 7

8. Make a same-size drawing of the decoration, on typewriter paper, then cut it out. Pat out a ⅛-inch-thick slab of clay, large enough for two Tudor (wild rose) decorations. Place the paper over the clay, and with the point of a small knife, cut around the edges of the pattern; repeat for the second decoration. Curl the edges of the petals back toward the center. With a thin nail or skewer point, incise the clay to form the petals. Build up the center with a small piece of clay to form the raised area (see drawing).

Step 8

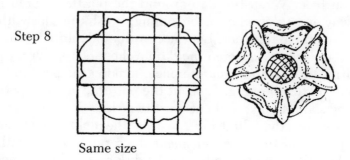

Same size

9. Put clay slip on the back of each decoration and on the center area of the front and back of the mug. Carefully press each decoration in place, smoothing the joining with the plastic tool.

10. Let the mug dry to leather hard, then smooth out any rough surfaces, inside and out with the wire tool and damp sponge.

11. Allow the mug to dry thoroughly for three or four days before baking. When completely dry, smooth the surface with sandpaper if necessary.

12. Bake the mug in the oven following directions in Chapter 4.

13. See Chapter 4 for directions for glazing and painting the surface. When the mug is completely cold, add the white air-dried glaze or acrylic paint, on the outside only, brushing it on lightly in horizontal strokes. You can cover the decorations and the handle, but be sure that no dribbles of paint run down the sides of the mug. When the white covering has dried, color the inside of the mug with a light tan (white paint and brown paint mixed together) air-dried glaze or paint. Bring the tan color over the top, and add a ¼-inch border on the outside top of the mug. Also cover the two side decorations with blue air-dried glaze or acrylic paint. Let the tan and blue coats dry completely.

14. When the colors are completely dry, cover the acrylic paint, inside and out, with acrylic polymer matte medium. If you have used air-dried glaze, there is no need for a clear glaze covering. Let mug dry thoroughly before using it—but remember it cannot be used for liquids.

PRIMITIVE COOKING POT

In the Winchester Cathedral treasure room, there is a tenth- to eleventh-century clay cooking pot made of a gritty terra-cotta clay. It is shaped somewhat like the pot from a very much earlier period—the Warring States in China. Since the opening is narrow in proportion to the ten-inch-high pot, it might have been used to cook porridge or soup that would be poured out in a semi-liquid state. The bottom and sides still show soot marks from the fire.

Your project pot is half the size of the original, and just as irregularly shaped. Build up the pot with coils, without using a template, just by following the drawing with your eyes and hands to make the final pot, as the English potter did so many centuries ago. Of course, you cannot cook with this pot or store food in it, but it makes a nice addition to your pottery collection.

Materials and Tools
ruler
oven-baked clay, approximately 1 pound
tools and supplies (Chapter 2)
air-dried glaze or acrylic paint, terra-cotta color
acrylic polymer matte medium
flat watercolor brush—¾ inch wide (for air-dried glaze)
flat nylon brush—¾ inch wide (for acrylic paint and medium)

Directions
1. First read the directions in Chapter 3 for making a coil pot.

2. Pat out a clay disk, 1½ inches in diameter and ⅜ inches thick; center the disk on a plaster bat or tile.

3. Build up the pot with clay coils ⅜ inch in diameter, starting on the outside of the disk (see drawing), as there is no foot on this pot. Check the shape of the pot with the drawing. This pot is 5 inches high, 5 inches in diameter at its widest point, and the top opening is 2½ inches in diameter. Set the pot aside to stiffen until leather hard.

4. When the pot is leather hard, go over the surface with a damp sponge, then set the pot aside again for several days to dry thoroughly.

5. Bake the pot in the oven following the directions in Chapter 4.

6. After the pot has been baked and cooled, cover the surfaces with the terra-cotta color, using the flat ¾-inch brush. Let the color dry. If you have used acrylic paint, then add a coat of acrylic polymer matte medium over the dry terra-cotta color and let dry. The glaze does not need a covering coat.

France

INTERLOCKING TILES

In Europe, house floors are usually covered with plain or decorated clay tiles. Shapes and designs vary from country to country, and century to century. The outlines of individual tiles are not always squares, but are cleverly designed shapes that fit into each other. The painted designs on individual tiles sometimes form a larger design which includes several tiles.

This project is based on the interlocking shape of an eighteenth-century French floor tile made of terra-cotta clay. You can make a single tile to hold a hot dish or a potted plant on a tabletop. Or you can make four tiles to show how the design fits together and use them to hold a table centerpiece. The edging design is just a narrow incised line; an alternate can be a border made with a thin wash of white paint or glaze with some of the terra-cotta color showing through. If oven-baked terra-cotta clay is not available, use the lighter tan clays and then color the baked tiles a terra-cotta color.

Materials and Tools
typewriter paper, pencil, ruler, scissors (for pattern)
oven-baked terra-cotta clay or any oven-baked clay,
    approximately 1 pound
tools and other supplies (Chapter 2)
clear air-dried glaze (for terra-cotta clay)
acrylic paint, rust color, white (see *Variation*)
acrylic polymer matte medium
flat watercolor brush, ¾ inch wide (for air-dried glaze)
flat nylon brush, ¾ inch wide (for acrylic paint and medium)

Directions
  1. First, read the directions in Chapter 3 for making Clay Tiles.
  2. Enlarge the tile pattern on the typewriter paper to the size

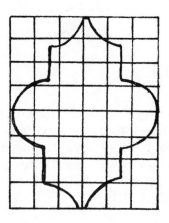

Step 2

Enlarge squares

you want. See Chapter 2 (Enlarging a Pattern). Cut out the pattern and set aside.

3. Roll out sufficient clay for one or more tiles, ½-inch thick.

4. Lay the paper pattern over the clay slab, and cut around the edges with the point of a small knife. Carefully remove the excess clay from around the edges of the tile or tiles. Let the tiles dry without disturbing them until stiff enough to lift up without spoiling the shape.

5. Then cut out the bottom foot (see Chapter 3, Cutting a Foot). Also cut a thin, shallow line, no more than ⅟₁₆-inch wide and deep, and ¼-inch in from the top edges.

6. Let the clay dry until leather hard, then smooth the surfaces with a damp sponge.

7. After several days, when completely dry, bake in the oven following directions in Chapter 4 (Baking Clay).

8. After the tile or tiles have been baked and cooled, cover the terra-cotta clay with clear, air-dried glaze or acrylic polymer matte medium, and set aside to dry. See Chapter 4 for directions on glazing or painting the tiles.

9. If you have used a clay which bakes to a light tan color, then add a covering of a rust-colored, air-dried glaze or acrylic paint over all the surfaces. The acrylic paint when dry will need a coat of acrylic polymer matte medium.

Variation
On either the terra-cotta clay tiles or those which have been painted a rust color, you can add a ¼- to ⅜-inch-wide band of a thin wash of white paint before covering the tile with a coat of acrylic polymer matte medium, or clear air-dried glaze.

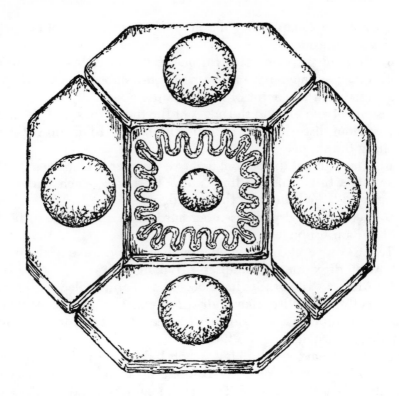

SIX-SIDED TILES

These six-sided eighteenth-century floor tiles are covered with a light blue glaze, with a center circle of darker blue. They can be arranged in different combinations, including one that centers around a square tile. You can choose your own combination of colors and designs for these clay tiles.

Materials and Tools
typewriter paper, pencil, ruler, scissors, compass
oven-baked clay, approximately 1 pound
tools and other supplies (Chapter 2)
acrylic paint or air-dried glaze, light blue and dark blue
acrylic polymer gloss medium
flat watercolor brush, ¾ inch wide (for air-dried glaze)
flat nylon brush, ¾ inch wide (for acrylic paint and medium)

Directions

1. First read the directions in Chapter 3 for making Clay Tiles.

2. Enlarge the tile pattern or patterns on the typewriter paper to the size you want (see Chapter 2, Enlarging a Pattern). Cut out the pattern or patterns and set aside.

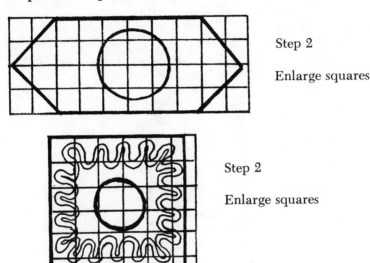

Step 2

Enlarge squares

Step 2

Enlarge squares

3. Roll out sufficient clay for one or more tiles, ½ inch thick.

4. Lay the paper pattern or patterns over the clay slab, and cut around the edges with the point of a small knife. Carefully remove the excess clay from around the edges of the tile or tiles. Let the clay dry without disturbing the tiles until they are stiff enough to lift up without spoiling the shape.

5. Then cut out the bottom foot (see Chapter 3, Cutting a Foot). Let the clay dry until leather hard, then smooth the surfaces with a damp sponge.

6. After setting tiles aside for several days until completely dry, bake them in the oven following directions in Chapter 4, Baking Clay.

7. After the tile or tiles have been baked and cooled, cover the top and sides with pale blue air-dried glaze or acrylic paint. See Chapter 4 for directions on glazing or painting the tiles. Let dry thoroughly.

8. With the compass draw a circle in the middle of each six-sided tile. Fill in the circle with the dark blue air-dried glaze or acrylic paint. If you are using the rectangular tile as the center of a design using several tiles, then fill in the squiggly lines with dark blue paint and add a small circle in the center (see drawing). Set tiles aside to dry.

9. If you have used acrylic paint to cover and decorate the tiles, then add a final coat of acrylic polymer gloss medium on the top, sides, and bottom of the tiles. Set aside to dry thoroughly.

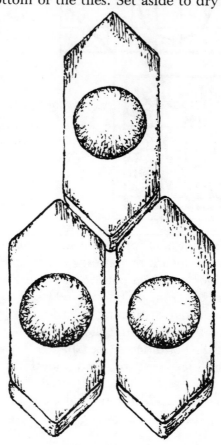

Greece

OWL CUP

This is a black-glazed, terra-cotta clay wine cup, made in the fourth to fifth century B.C. in the area of the Greek colonies in southern Italy on the Adriatic coast, in what is now known as Apulia. The cup is part of a large collection of Greek vases, plates and cups of all types which had been dug up in this area and are now permanently exhibited in the Jatta Museum at Ruvo, Italy.

You can make this small cup, only 3½ inches high, from oven-baked terra-cotta clay (or any type of oven-baked clay), using either the slab or coil method. For the slab method, your mold will be a round-bottomed jelly glass or custard cup. The clay must be rolled very thin—barely ¼ inch thick. If using coils ¼ inch in diameter, then make a template.

Materials and Tools
typewriter paper, cardboard, carbon paper,
   ruler, pencil, scissors
oven-baked terra-cotta clay or any oven-baked clay,
glass jelly mold or custard cup
air-dried glaze or acrylic paint, black, rust (optional)
acrylic polymer matte medium

flat, ¾ inch wide, and round #4 and #2 watercolor brushes
(for air-dried glaze)
flat, ¾ inch wide, and round #4 and #2 nylon brushes
(for acrylic paint)

Directions
Slab Method

1. Follow directions in Chapter 3 for rolling out a clay slab ¼ inch thick, preparing the mold, forming, and drying the clay on the mold.

2. While the clay is drying on the mold, roll out two coils for the handles, each 3 inches long and approximately ⅜ inch in diameter. Also roll out a third coil of the same thickness and long enough to circle the bottom of the cup. Place all three coils in a small plastic bag so they will stay moist enough to form into the handles and bottom of the cup.

3. When the cup has been removed from the mold, attach the third coil to the bottom of the cup with slip. Smooth out the joining and flatten and smooth the coil to an outward flare (see drawing). Curve the two other coils into loops and attach them with slip to the top of the cup—on opposite sides. Set the cup aside to dry until leather hard, then smooth the surfaces inside and out with a damp sponge and wire tool. Let dry completely before baking.

Coil Method

1. Enlarge the template pattern onto the cardboard and cut it out with the scissors. Follow the directions in Chapter 2 for enlarging a pattern.

Step 1—Coil Method

Enlarge to ½" squares

Template, discard dotted area

2. Pat out a clay disk, 1¾ inches in diameter and ½ inch thick, and center it on a plaster bat or tile.

3. Build up the cup with coils of clay ¼ inch in diameter, checking the shape with the template. Read the directions in Chapter 3 for forming a coil pot. The cup's final size is 3½ inches high and 2¾ inches in diameter at the top rim.

4. Roll out two coils for the handles, each 3 inches long and approximately ⅜ inch in diameter. Curve the two coils into loops and attach them with slip to the top of the cup—on opposite sides.

5. Cut out the foot (see Chapter 3, Cutting a Foot). Curve the sides of the foot into an outward flare (see drawing).

6. Set the cup aside to dry until leather hard, then smooth the surfaces, inside and out with a damp sponge and wire tool. Let dry completely before baking in the oven.

7. Glazing or painting the cup is the same whether it is made by the slab or coil method. Read and follow the directions for glazing or painting in Chapter 4.

8. Enlarge the design on the typewriter paper; see directions for enlarging patterns in Chapter 2. Transfer the design to opposite sides of the cup (the sides without handles), using carbon paper.

Step 8

Enlarge to ½" squares

9. Color the inside of the cup with black air-dried glaze or acrylic paint, using the flat ¾-inch brush. Fill in the background on the outside of the cup with black air-dried glaze or acrylic paint, painting around the plants and owls so they are left in the terra-cotta color of the clay. Use the round #4 and #2 brushes for this work, filling in the lines of wing, eyes, and beak of the owl with the black color. Finally color the handles with either the black air-dried glaze or acrylic paint. Let dry thoroughly.

10. If you have used acrylic paint for the color, then cover the inside and outside surfaces with acrylic polymer matte medium as a final finish. The air-dried glaze does not need this additional cover.

11. Set the cup aside for several days to dry completely.

Variation

If you used a gray or pale tan clay, then after the cup has been baked, cover the outside of the cup with a rust-colored air-dried glaze or acrylic paint. When this coat is completely dry, then follow the instructions in Steps 8 through 11, for transferring the design and adding the black color.

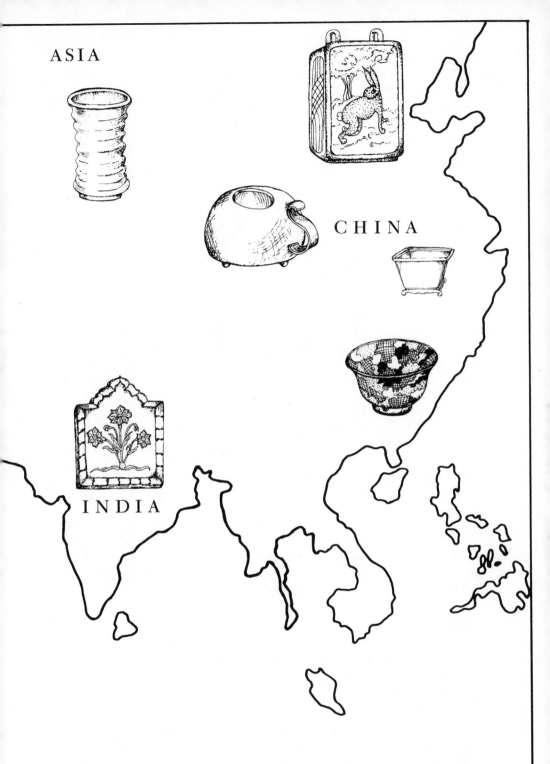

China, India, and other Asian countries have given the world
beautiful clay objects in many shapes and colors.

India

FLOWERED TILE

A delicate, make-believe flower is drawn in the center of this border tile. This was a favorite form of decoration of the Mughal period around 1625 A.D. in India. Red flowers stand out against a white background. The stems and leaves are a soft gray-green which is also the color of the border, accented with red lines.

Materials and Tools
typewriter paper, pencil, scissors, carbon paper
oven-baked clay, approximately 1 pound
tools and other supplies (Chapter 2)
air-dried glaze or acrylic paint, white, red, light green, black
acrylic polymer gloss medium
flat, ¾ inch wide, and round #4 and #2 watercolor brushes
  (for air-dried glaze)

flat, ¾ inch wide, and round #4 and #2 nylon brushes
(for acrylic paint and medium)

Directions
1. First, read the directions in Chapter 3 for making Clay Tiles.
2. Transfer the tile pattern to the typewriter paper by the

Step 2, Tile Shape   Same size

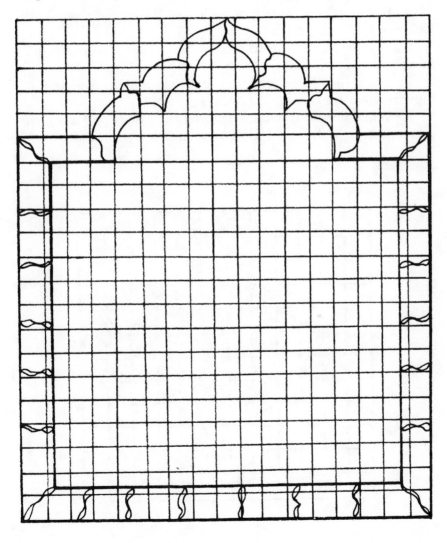

grid method (see Chapter 2, Enlarging, Reducing, and Transferring Designs). Cut out the pattern with the scissors and set aside.

3. Roll out sufficient clay for the tile, which should be $4\frac{1}{4} \times 5\frac{1}{4}$ inches, and $\frac{1}{2}$ inch thick.

4. Lay the paper pattern over the clay slab, and cut around the edges with the point of a small knife. Carefully remove the excess clay from around the edges of the tile. Also remove the paper pattern. Let the tile dry without disturbing it until it is stiff enough to lift up without spoiling the shape.

5. Cut out the bottom foot with the wire modeling tool (see Chapter 3, Cutting a Foot).

6. Let the clay dry until leather hard, then smooth the surfaces with a damp sponge.

7. When the tile is completely dry, bake it in the oven following directions for baking in Chapter 4.

8. While the tile is baking, transfer the flower pattern to the typewriter paper by the grid method as before. Set aside.

Step 8, Tile Design   Same size

9. When the tile has been baked and cooled, cover the top and sides with either white air-dried glaze or acrylic paint using the ¾-inch flat brush. See Chapter 4 for directions on glazing or painting the tile. Let the white covering dry completely.

10. When dry, transfer the flower pattern and the border around the edge to the tile with carbon paper. Color the petals of the flowers with either red air-dried glaze or acrylic paint, leaving the petal edges white. Use the #4 and #2 brushes. Do not color the centers of the flowers. When the red has dried, add a little white to the green, and just a touch of red to dull the color. With either the #4 and #2 brush add the green to the stems and leaves, and to the centers of the flowers. Fill in the border around the edge of the tile with the green using the #4 brush. Let all the colors dry until hard.

11. Finally, with black and the #2 brush add the lines that separate and outline the petals, plus the center lines of each petal. Repeat with the black in the center of each leaf. You may have to retransfer these lines from the original drawing using carbon paper. Also add the squiggly lines to the border using the red color. Set the tile aside for several days to dry completely.

12. If you have used acrylic paint, then cover the sides and top with the acrylic polymer gloss medium; the air-dried glaze will not need this coat. When the medium is dry, turn the tile over and cover the back with the medium. Set aside to dry.

Italy

FISH CANDLE HOLDER

This sixteenth-century, fish-shaped candle holder was made in
Ferrara, a city in northern Italy. Ferrara was at the center of the
Renaissance movement, a very creative period in architecture,
art, and literature, which began before 1100 A.D. and lasted for
several centuries. The candle holder made so long ago, was eight
inches long, covered with a tan glaze splashed with blue. For this
project the size has been reduced to six inches. The fish is formed
with coils as an upright "vase," then turned on its side, and placed
on a clay support disk, with candle holder, handles, and tail added.

Materials and Tools
lightweight cardboard, pencil, ruler, scissors
oven-baked clay, approximately 1 pound
tools and other supplies (Chapter 2)
candle, ½ to ⅝ inch base diameter
air-dried glaze or acrylic paint, tan, blue

acrylic polymer gloss medium
flat, ¾ inch wide, and round #4 watercolor brushes
   (for air-dried glazes)
flat, ¾ inch wide, and round #4 nylon brushes
   (for acrylic paint and medium)

Directions
   1. First, read the directions in Chapter 3 for forming a coil pot.
   2. Enlarge the template pattern onto the cardboard; cut out the pattern with scissors. Follow the directions in Chapter 2 for enlarging the pattern.

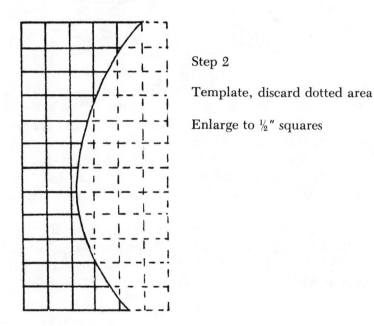

Step 2

Template, discard dotted area

Enlarge to ½″ squares

   3. Pat out 2 clay disks—½ × ¼ inches and 1¾ × ½ inches. Center the ½-inch disk on a plaster bat or tile. Place the 1¾-inch disk in a plastic bag to keep the clay moist until the fish shape has been built up with coils.
   4. Build up the fish shape with coils ⅜ inch in diameter, attaching the first coil at the *side* of the clay disk as you will not be

forming a foot. As you add coils, check the shape with the template, and make sure the shape is centered. The top opening is ½ inch. Smooth the surface with the sponge before removing the fish from the bat.

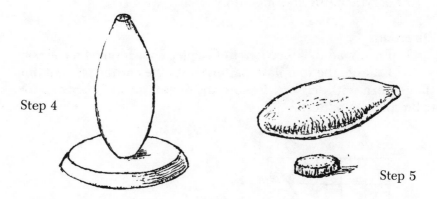

Step 4

Step 5

5. Remove the 1¾-inch disk from the plastic bag. Hold the fish to one side, and place the disk in the center of the bat. Lay the fish on the disk, just off center so that the head area is nearest to the disk (see drawing). Add a coil ⅛ inch in diameter between the fish and the disk. Smooth with slip and the rounded end of the plastic tool to make a firm bond between fish and disk. Then cut away enough clay on each side of the disk to form it into a long oval.

6. At the head end of the fish, carefully scrape off some of the clay with the wire modeling tool to shape the nose, adding a little more clay if needed. Scoop out a shallow oval on each side for the eyes (see drawings).

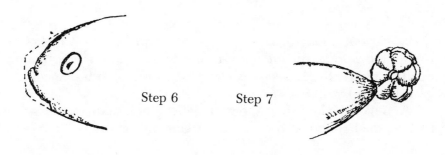

Step 6   Step 7

7. Squeeze and pull the clay around the ½-inch opening at the other end of the fish to close the opening and form a point. To make the tail, pat and pinch out a thin disk only ⅛-inch thick and 1 inch in diameter. Make a small indentation in the center and attach the disk to the pointed end of the fish, using slip and a thin roll of clay. Flute the edges of the disk (see drawing).

8. Cut out a circle ⅜ inch in diameter in the center of the top of the fish. The hole should be centered above the supporting disk on the bottom of the fish (see drawing).

9. Roll or pat out a ¼-inch-thick strip, 1½ × 4¼ inches for the candle holder. Curve the strip around into a 1-inch-diameter tube as you place it in position around the hole. Attach with slip and a thin coil of clay, smoothing the bottom to follow the shape of the fish. There will be a "shelf" of clay between the hole and the inner wall of the tube.

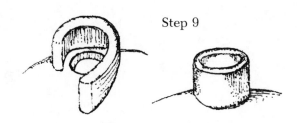

Step 9

10. For the handles, you will make two clay strips, ⅛ inch thick, ½ inch wide, and 4½ inches long. Curve them outward on each side of the tube, squeezing and pointing the end that is attached to the side of the fish, using slip and smoothing both ends with the plastic tool (see drawing).

11. Add a coil of clay, thicker in the center and thinned to a point at each end to curve over the top of the fish and partway down the sides, just behind the eyes. Follow the drawing for placement.

12. Let the fish dry until leather hard. Cut a foot in the disk (see Chapter 3). Then if needed smooth the surface of the fish with a damp sponge. Set the candle holder aside for several days to dry completely.

13. Bake in the oven following directions in Chapter 4. Remove from oven and cool.

14. Cover fish, candle holder, handles, and base with the tan air-dried glaze or acrylic paint, using the flat ¾-inch brush. Let dry well. Then add splashes of blue glaze or paint on the surface of the fish. Outline the eye with blue and put in the vertical eye pupil, plus two little blue dots at each side of the nose. Use the round #4 brush (see Chapter 4 for directions). Let dry completely.

15. If you have used acrylic paint, then add a final clear coat of acrylic polymer gloss medium over the whole fish, with the flat ¾-inch brush. Let dry for several days.

Martinique

PIERCED-PATTERN CANDLE HOLDERS

In Martinique, where windows and porches in the homes and in restaurant dining rooms are open all year round, burning candles are protected from the wind by clay cylinders, pierced with a pattern and set over a clay saucer which holds the candle. The flickering shadows cast by the candle flame dance against the walls forming patterns of light and dark.

Materials and Tools
typewriter paper, pencil, ruler, scissors, compass (for pattern)
oven-baked clay, approximately 1 pound
a straight-sided can or bottle, 6 inches high
   × 3 inches in diameter, for a mold
tools and other supplies (Chapter 2)
air-dried clear glaze or acrylic polymer gloss medium
flat watercolor brush, ¾ inch wide (for air-dried glaze)
flat nylon brush, ¾ inch wide (for acrylic medium)

Directions

1. First read the directions in Chapter 3 for forming Slab Pots.

2. Enlarge one of the patterns, or if you are making several candle holders, then enlarge the other two patterns. Cut out the

Step 2   Enlarge to 1″ squares

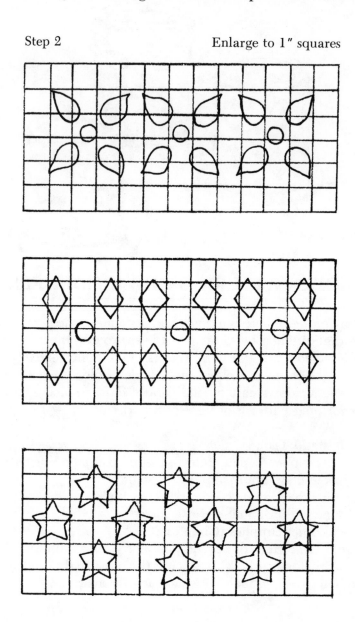

holes of the designs. See the directions for Enlarging Patterns in Chapter 2. Draw a circle with the compass, 3 inches wider than the diameter of the mold; this is the pattern for the saucer.

3. Roll out a slab of clay that is ½ inch thick and 6 inches wide. It has to be long enough to form both the cylinder and the saucer. Measure the circumference of the mold with a length of string and add an extra inch.

4. When the clay slab is slightly stiff, lay the cylinder pattern over the clay, and cut out the openings with the point of a small knife. Carefully remove the cut-out pieces. Lay the saucer pattern over the rest of the clay slab, and cut out the circle. Remove excess clay from around the circle.

5. When the patterned slab is stiff enough to lift up, but not so stiff that it cannot be curved around the mold, remove it from the plastic work surface. Wrap the slab around the plastic-covered mold; cut away any excess clay at the joining; brush the ends with slip, smoothing them together. Let the clay dry only until it will stand alone, then remove the mold.

6. While the cylinder is drying, loosen the circle of clay. Form a rope of clay, ½ inch in diameter and long enough to fit around the outside edge of the circle. Smear slip around the top edge of the circle. Put the clay rope in place, smoothing and straightening the sides and top so that it is no longer a "rope" shape. This edging and the sides of the circle should be even, and the inside joining smooth. Cut a foot in the bottom of the saucer (see Chapter 3). Let dry.

7. When both the cylinder and the saucer are leather hard, smooth the surfaces with the wire tool and moist sponge. Let dry several days until hard, and if necessary go over the surfaces with sandpaper.

8. Bake the cylinder and the saucer in the oven, following directions in Chapter 4.

9. When the cylinder and the saucer are cool, cover all surfaces with clear air-dried glaze or acrylic polymer gloss medium. Let dry undisturbed until the surfaces are hard and dry. See Chapter 4 for painting directions.

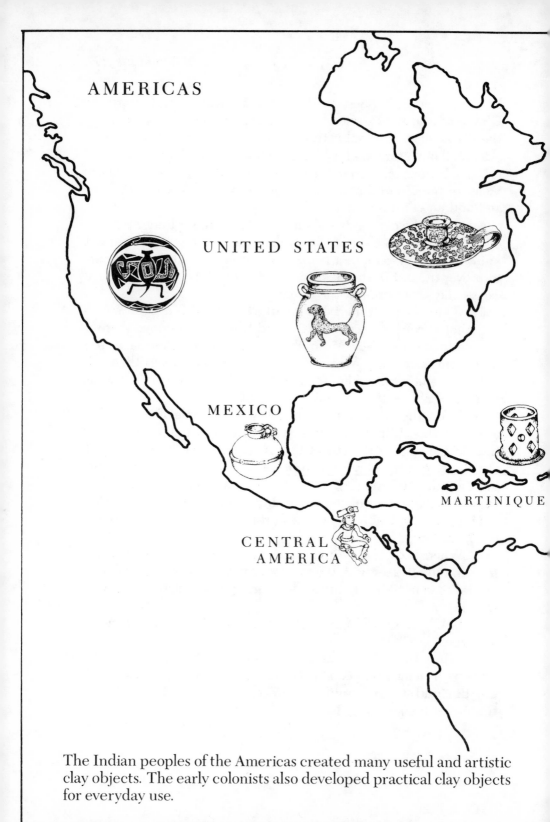

AMERICAS

UNITED STATES

MEXICO

CENTRAL
AMERICA

MARTINIQUE

The Indian peoples of the Americas created many useful and artistic clay objects. The early colonists also developed practical clay objects for everyday use.

Mexico and Central America

MAYAN FIGURE

The Mayan civilization flourished in Mexico on the Yucatan peninsula as early as the fifth century A.D. and earlier throughout Central America and parts of Mexico. The Mayans were farmers and builders, stone masons and carvers, potters and weavers, and worked precious metals and semiprecious stones. Their clay was a warm tan to a terra-cotta brown in color; their clay pots and figures were often unglazed. In this project, the small figure is covered with a clear "glaze" to strengthen the surface, and to keep the clay surface from dusting off.

This is a simple figure to make, as head, arms, body, and legs are made with coils of clay, and put together with clay slip.

Materials and Tools
oven-baked clay, ½ pound
tools and other supplies (Chapter 2)
acrylic polymer matte medium
round #4 nylon brush

Directions
   1. Read the directions in Chapter 3 for rolling out clay coils.
   2. Following these directions roll out the following coils: *one*, 1 inch long × 1¼ inch in diameter for the head; *one*, ¼ inch long × ⅜ inch in diameter for the neck; *one*, 2 inches long × ½ inch in diameter for the body; *two*, 2¾ inches long × ¼ inch in diameter for the arms; *two*, 3¼ inches long × ⅜ inch in diameter for the legs; *one*, 2⅝ inches long × ³⁄₁₆ inch in diameter for the neck roll; *one*, 2¾ inches long × by ³⁄₁₆ inch in diameter for the waist roll. In addition, pinch and pat out a strip of clay for the headpiece, ⅜ inch wide, ⅓ inch thick, and 4¼ inches long. You will also need other little balls and tiny strips of clay as decorations on headpiece, arms, and legs, but these can be pinched out as needed following the figure drawing for approximate size and placement.

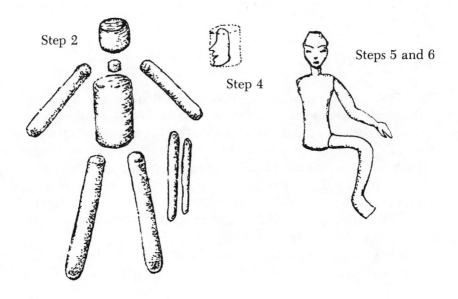

Step 2

Step 4

Steps 5 and 6

3. In the following steps, refer constantly to the drawings for this project.

4. You will need only ½ the thickness of the head coil. Cut it in half vertically; with a toothpick carve out the features, adding bits of clay where needed for the nose or chin.

5. Attach the head to the neck coil with slip. Add the body coil, trimming and squeezing it so it is thinned into the waist and is narrower and flatter from front to back than it is wide. Add the arms to the top of the body coil, smoothing them into shoulders, then bend the coil at the elbows, and form the hands with a toothpick.

6. Add the two leg coils at the bottom sides of the body, smoothing them into hips. Bend the legs at the knee and pinch the ends into feet.

7. With the wire modeling tool, scrape the clay on the back of the body to form a very straight, flat back.

8. Add the neck roll, smoothing it into the back of the neck. Add the waist roll, leaving it fully rounded across the back.

9. Put thin coils around the wrists with a little circle of clay on top of the roll—a bracelet giving the effect of a wristwatch. Also add the leg decorations below the knee.

10. Finally, fold the head decoration strip in half by bringing the two ends together in the center of the back of the strip. Cut away some of the top of the head coil, and fit the strip into place over the top of the head. Add the center circles of clay, as well as the two ear circles.

11. Adjust the arms and legs so the figure is balanced in a sitting position with heels on a level with the bottom of the body.

12. Allow the figure to dry until leather hard, then go over the surface with a damp sponge to smooth the surface. Let figure dry completely.

13. Bake the figure in the oven following directions in Chapter 4.

14. When the figure has been baked and cooled, cover all surfaces with the acrylic polymer matte medium and let dry for several days.

PRE-COLUMBIAN PITCHER

Many clay pots, made many centuries ago in Mexico, Central and South America, cannot be dated for an exact year, so they are identified as Pre-Columbian. That is, made before Columbus discovered the Western continents. The original pitcher which we are going to copy is 6½ inches high, made of terra-cotta clay covered with a dull glaze, and comes from the area of the Costa Grande tribe in Mexico.

If you cannot find oven-baked clay in terra-cotta color, use an available clay, then paint the finished baked pitcher with rust-red glaze or acrylic paint. The size of the pitcher depends on the size of the two matching bowls (used as molds) which are available to you. See suggested size in the list below, then follow the drawings and adjust all proportions accordingly.

Materials and Tools
oven-baked clay, approximately 1 pound
2 bowl forms, approximately 5 inches in diameter,
   2¼ inches high
tools and other supplies (Chapter 2)
acrylic paint, or air-dried glaze—rust color
acrylic polymer matte medium
flat watercolor brush, ¾ inch wide (for air-dried glaze)
flat nylon brush, ¾ inch wide (for acrylic paint
   and medium)

Directions

1. First, read the directions in Chapter 3 for forming Slab Pots.

2. You will need two slabs of clay, each one large enough to cover the outside of the two bowl forms; a 2 × 6½-inch strip for the pitcher top; a ½ × 3-inch strip for the handle. You will also need a roll of clay ⅜ inch in diameter, long enough to stretch around the middle of the pitcher.

3. Prepare the bowl forms and cover them with the rolled clay slab (see Chapter 3).

4. After the bowls have been covered with the clay slabs, cut out a 2-inch-in-diameter round hole from the center of one of the clay bowls. Allow the bowls to dry until the clay is stiff enough to be removed from the forms, but do not let it dry until it is hard, as the clay will shrink and split.

5. To put the two halves of the pitcher together, scratch the matching edges of the two clay bowls with a knife. Smear clay slip over the scratch marks. Put the edges of the two bowls together and smooth the outside surface of the joint. With the flat end of the plastic tool, reach inside the pitcher through the top hole and smooth the joint as best you can. Flatten the bottom of the pitcher, as a foot will not be added to this pot.

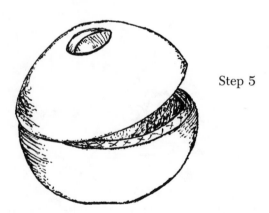

Step 5

6. Scratch a ¼-inch-wide area around the edge of the round opening; smear clay slip over the scratch marks. Curl the 2 × 6½-inch clay strip around the opening, pressing the edge into the

clay slip. Smooth the joint between this upright neck and the body of the pitcher; also smooth the vertical joint of the two ends of the strip. At the top edge pull a "lip" forward with thumb and forefinger. Pinch clay into two "bumps" to form a pouring guide.

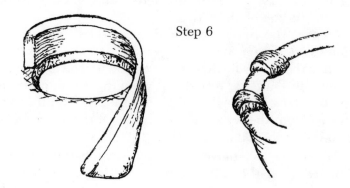

Step 6

7. Add the handle on the side opposite the lip, holding the ½ × 3-inch strip in place with slip—see drawing for placement. Smooth both ends into the clay of the pitcher. Add small rounds of clay as decorations.

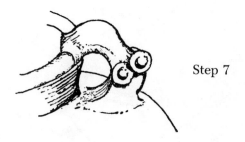

Step 7

8. Roll out a rope of clay following the directions in Chapter 3, Coil Pots. The rope should be long enough to go around the middle of the pitcher to cover the joining of the two halves. Smear clay slip over the joint surface; add clay slip to one side of the clay rope. Press the rope into position, smoothing a little of each side against the body of the pitcher. With an index finger, make an indentation in the rope at even intervals all around its length.

9. Allow the pitcher to partially dry, then smooth the surfaces with tools and a damp sponge. Let the clay pitcher dry thoroughly for several days before baking.

10. Before baking the pitcher in the oven, read the directions in Chapter 4, then bake the pitcher.

11. If necessary, color the surface of the baked pitcher with either rust-colored acrylic paint or air-dried glaze; let dry. When dry, cover the acrylic paint with clear acrylic polymer matte medium. If using air-dried glaze, you may want to add a second coat. Let the pitcher stand, undisturbed, until the surface is completely dry. See Chapter 4 for the directions for both these processes.

Persia

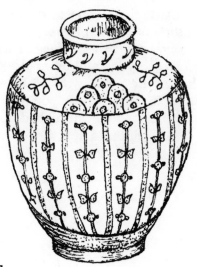

ANCIENT VASE

This dark blue-green, eighteenth-century vase is decorated with black brush-stroke designs. The original, which is in the ceramic museum in Faenza, Italy, is approximately eleven inches tall. In this project, the height has been reduced to six inches to make it easier to form and bake the vase.

Make the vase in two parts with coils, then upend the shallower bowl onto the deeper bottom, holding the two halves together with slip. The brush design can be applied freehand, or you can enlarge the design, transferring it as a repeated design to the baked vase.

Materials and Tools
typewriter paper, pencil, ruler, scissors
carbon paper
lightweight cardboard

oven-baked clay, approximately 1 pound
tools and other supplies (Chapter 2)
air-dried glaze or acrylic paint, blue-green, black
acrylic polymer gloss medium
flat, ¾ inch wide, and round #4 and #2
    watercolor brushes (for air-dried glaze)
flat, ¾ inch wide, and round #4 and #2
    nylon brushes (for acrylic paint)

Directions

    1. First read the directions in Chapter 3 for forming a coil pot.

    2. Enlarge the template patterns for a 6-inch-high vase (Steps 4 to 6 for measurements) onto the cardboard and cut them out. Follow directions in Chapter 2 for enlarging a pattern.

Top   Templates, discard dotted areas

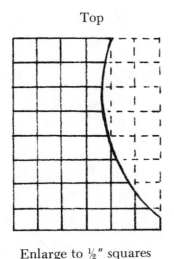

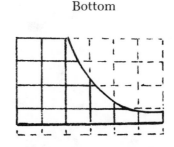

Bottom

Enlarge to ½" squares   Enlarge to ½" squares

    3. Pat out a disk of clay that is 1½ inches in diameter and ½ inch thick for the bottom of the vase. Center the disk on a clay bat or tile.

    4. Start building up the larger, lower part of the vase with coils, checking the shape with the template. When it has reached

a height of 4 inches and the rim is 3½ inches in diameter, set the pot aside in a closed plastic bag.

5. Pat or roll out a ¼-inch-thick strip of clay, ½ × 7 inches. Curve it into an upright cylinder 2 inches in diameter, smoothing the joining with clay slip. Temporarily this will be the bottom of a shallow bowl, but in the end will be the mouth of the vase.

6. On top of the clay cylinder build up the shallow bowl to 1½ inches high and 3½ inches in diameter at its top rim, following procedures in Step 4. Cut out a circle 1½ inch in diameter in the center of the bowl, to match the opening in the clay cylinder.

7. Scratch around both rims with a knife point or nail. Smear the scratched area with clay slip, and upend the shallow bowl onto the larger base bowl. Smooth the joining inside and out with slip and the plastic tool. Set the vase aside until leather hard.

Step 7

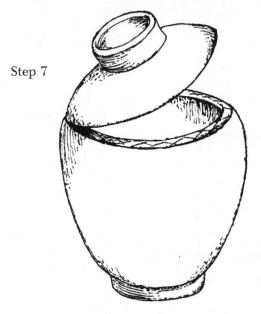

8. Cut out the foot at the bottom of the vase, following directions in Chapter 3.

9. Smooth the vase with a damp sponge and the wire tool. Smooth and level the top opening. Set the vase aside for several days to dry completely—then go over the whole surface with sandpaper if necessary.

10. When the clay is dry, bake the vase in the oven, following directions in Chapter 4.

11. When the vase has been baked and cooled cover the outside of the vase, including the inside of the mouth with blue-green air-dried glaze or acrylic paint using the flat brush and following directions in Chapter 4. Set the vase aside to dry thoroughly before adding the black decorations.

12. While the blue-green glaze or paint is drying, enlarge the design patterns on the typewriter paper, following directions in Chapter 2. Transfer the patterns to the vase with carbon paper; plan an equal number of vertical lines around the lower half of the vase. With the round #4 and #2 brushes paint the lines first, then allow to dry before adding the "sprigged" design to avoid smearing the paint. The scallop pattern is repeated on opposite sides of the "shoulder" of the vase with the sprigged patterns in-between. The outside edge of the foot and 1 inch of the vase above the foot is colored solid black. You can also work freehand, following the designs of the patterns.

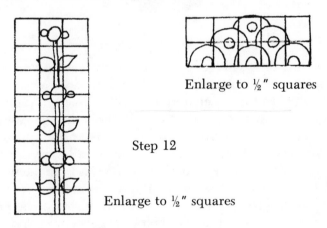

Enlarge to ½" squares

Step 12

Enlarge to ½" squares

13. When the black designs are thoroughly dry, cover the whole vase and the inside of the mouth with acrylic polymer gloss medium *if it has been painted with acrylic paints.* The air-dried glaze does not need a covering. In either case, paint the inside of the foot with the acrylic polymer gloss medium. Set vase aside to dry completely.

Portugal

GOBLET

Albufeira, a fishing village on the southern coast of Portugal, almost seems to be a north African village. Its narrow streets spill down the cliffs to the beach and sea below. You will reproduce a noble goblet-shaped container from this area that has something very African about it, with its simple white and gray geometric design. The original was almost ten inches tall, but this project cuts the size down to five inches, an easier size to make with coils and to bake in a kitchen oven. This goblet is made from two coil pots, put together with slip after they are formed; the herringbone design is cut into the clay before it hardens completely.

Materials and Tools
lightweight cardboard, pencil, ruler, scissors
oven-baked clay, approximately 1 pound
tools and supplies (Chapter 2)
air-dried glaze or acrylic paint, white, gray
acrylic polymer matte medium

flat, ¾ inch wide, and #2 round watercolor brushes
   (for air-dried glaze)
flat, ¾ inch wide, and #2 round nylon brushes
   (for acrylic paint and medium)

Templates, discard dotted areas

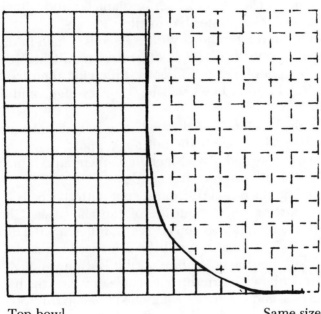

Top bowl   Same size

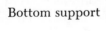
Bottom support

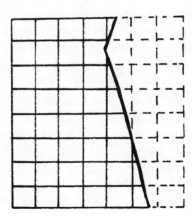

Same size

Directions

1. First read the directions in Chapter 3 for making a coil pot.

2. Transfer the two template patterns onto the cardboard by the grid method following directions in Chapter 2. Cut out the two templates with scissors.

3. Pat out a clay disk, 1 inch in diameter and ¼ inch thick; center the disk on a plaster bat or tile.

4. Build up the top bowl with clay coils ¼ inch in diameter, starting on the outside of the disk (see drawing). Check the shape with the template as you add coils, following the directions in Chapter 3. The final bowl will be 3 inches high, and 4 inches across the top.

5. Put the bowl inside a plastic bag to keep it moist while you make the second shape for the bottom support.

6. Pat out a second disk, 1 inch in diameter and ¼ inch thick; center the disk on a plaster bat or tile.

7. Build up the outward-slanting pot with clay coils ¼ inch in diameter, starting on the outside of the clay disk. Check the shape with the template as you add coils, following the directions in Chapter 3. The final pot will be 2 inches high and 2 inches across the top. Let the pot stiffen until it is strong enough to support the upper bowl. Turn the pot upside down on the bat. Level the top surface and scratch crosshatched lines on this top surface.

8. Remove the first bowl from the plastic bag, and separate it from its bat. Level its bottom and trim if necessary to match the bottom of the support pot. Mark the surface with crosshatched lines. Smear clay slip over the upturned top of the support pot, and place the bowl in position on top. Press lightly into place, and smooth the joining with the flat, rounded end of the plastic tool. Check all around to make sure the goblet is centered and the top of the bowl is trimmed evenly.

9. As soon as the clay is almost leather hard, go over the pot with a damp sponge to smooth all the surfaces, inside and out. Evenly measure out the four quarters on both the bowl and the support, making a light nick on the rim of the bowl and the bottom of the support. Lightly draw 4 vertical lines down the length of the bowl, and the support and perhaps a few slanting lines as a guide to the pattern. With the curved point of the wire modeling tool, carve out the herringbone pattern on the four sides of the bowl, leaving the top ¼ inch as a plain band. Also carve the pattern on the support, leaving a ¼-inch plain band at the bottom (see drawing).

10. Set the goblet aside for several days until completely dry, then go over the whole surface with sandpaper if necessary, removing also any leftover crumbles from carving the pattern.

11. Bake the bowl in the oven following directions in Chapter 4.

12. After the bowl has been baked and cooled, cover the inside and the outside surfaces with white air-dried glaze or acrylic paint, using the flat brush, following the glazing or painting directions in Chapter 4. Let the white surface dry completely.

13. With the round #4 brush, fill in the carved-out areas with light gray air-dried glaze or acrylic paint. Let dry. If you have used acrylic paint for the colors, then cover the inside and outside surfaces with the acrylic polymer matte medium as a final finish. The air-dried glaze does not need this additional cover. Let the goblet dry completely.

MOORISH PLATE

In the area around the Portuguese town of Evora there have always been many small potteries, where a family or a group share in the production of their craft. Some members form the pots, others are in charge of the kilns, still others develop the designs and do the decorating. This craft system allows the potters to create very individual designs—and to carry on a long tradition of careful potting and traditional as well as new designs.

Evora is a provincial capital, first settled in Roman times, then occupied by the Moors who left their imprint on the town with its whitewashed houses, and narrow alley-like streets. And many of the pottery designs and shapes show Moorish and other influences in the use of flowers, plant forms, and fanciful arabesques, often combined with simple drawings of animals and birds.

The original of this design is a platter, thirteen inches in diameter, but the project design has been reduced to eight inches, still keeping the deep center and wide flared edge.

Materials and Tools
typewriter paper, carbon paper, pencil, ruler, scissors, compass
oven-baked clay, approximately 1 pound
tools and other supplies (Chapter 2)
shallow soup plate, 8 inches in diameter, with a wide rim for a mold (see also *Variation*)
air-dried glaze or acrylic paint, white, chrome yellow, brown, prussian blue, olive-green
acrylic polymer matte medium
flat, ¾ inch wide, and round #4 and #2 watercolor brushes (for air-dried glaze)
flat, ¾ inch wide, and round #4 and #2 nylon brushes (for acrylic paint)

Directions
1. First, read the directions in Chapter 3 for making a slab bowl or plate.
2. Prepare the mold, then drape the clay slab over the bottom. Press the clay into place and trim the edges. Curve a coil ½ inch in diameter into a circle in the center of the back of the plate, as a foot. Smooth it into place with clay slip. Allow the clay to partially stiffen; remove from the mold as soon as the clay can be handled without spoiling its shape. Turn the clay plate right side up, and with the palms of your hands gently ease upward a 1½-inch rim around the edge, so that the edge is flared upward instead of being flat.
3. When the clay is leather hard, smooth the interior and exterior with a damp sponge and the wire tool.
4. Dry the plate thoroughly for several days, then bake it in the oven, following directions in Chapter 4.
5. While the clay is drying, enlarge the design pattern for the center and the rim on the typewriter paper, following enlarging directions in Chapter 2.

Step 5   Enlarge to ½-inch squares

Chrome yellow—small birds, lower half of large birds, gourds around edge.

Light Blue—upper half of large birds, half-circles on border, outer edge of plate, inner circle of plate.

Green—scalloped strips on border, all stems and pointed leaves.

Purple-red—zig-zag line, stems and round berries, bird outlines, gourd outlines, nest in middle, outlines of green scallops, and blue half-circles on border.

6. To decorate the plate, follow the glazing or painting directions in Chapter 4. Front and back of the plate are first covered with a warm cream color made by mixing a little of the chrome yellow and brown with the white glaze or paint. Use the flat ¾-inch-wide brush to apply the color to the plate. Let this coat dry thoroughly before adding the front design.

7. Transfer the pattern to the plate with carbon paper. Follow the color notes on the drawing, mixing colors if needed; dark blue and white together for a light blue; green and white together for a light green. First color the center section of the plate, as you will have to brace your hand on the rim of the plate. Use both the #4 and #2 round brushes for the decorations. Then add the rim decorations. When finished, let the glazed or painted colors dry completely.

8. If you have used acrylic paint, then cover the plate inside and out with acrylic polymer matte medium. Let dry thoroughly.

9. Display the plate on a wooden display rack, or if you want to prepare it to hang on the wall, see the chapter on the Southwest-Indian Bowl—*Variation*.

Variation

If you do not have a rimmed soup plate to use as a mold, then use a shallow bowl or deep saucer 5 inches in diameter as the center mold. Cut out a clay disk 8 inches in diameter, then cut and remove a center disk 4½ inches in diameter. When the shallow bowl is stiff enough to remove from its mold, transfer it to the center of the disk. With a thin roll of clay and slip attach the

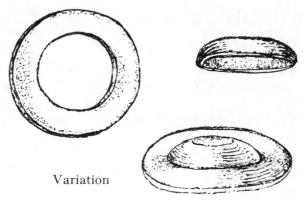

Variation

bowl to the rim; let both dry until they can be turned upright, then ease the 1½-inch rim up to form a flared edge. Moisten the inside joining with a damp sponge and smooth the rim joining into the bowl. Add a circle coil of clay as a foot. Follow the rest of the directions in Steps 4 through 9.

RED ROOSTER OF BARCELOS

In the Museum of Popular Art in Belem near Lisbon, Portugal, there are many sizes and designs of the Red Rooster of Barcelos, a river town near Braga in the north of Portugal. The cock represents an old legend concerning an innocent prisoner, sentenced to die who made a last plea to a judge who was having dinner. If he were innocent, he said, the baked rooster on the judge's plate would get up and crow—and up from the plate rose a red rooster with a mighty crow.

Follow the drawings in making a Barcelos rooster, painting it scarlet red with blue and white decorations. In this project it will be about 5 inches high, though many pottery cocks in Portugal are one to two feet high, and some are covered with elaborate designs.

Materials
ruler
oven-baked clay, approximately one pound
tools and supplies (Chapter 2)
air-dried glaze or acrylic paint, red, blue, white
acrylic polymer gloss medium
flat, ¾ inch wide, and #4 and #2 round watercolor brushes
   (for air-dried glaze)
flat, ¾ inch wide, and #4 and #2 round nylon brushes
   (for acrylic paint and medium)

Directions
1. As this is a sculptured object, made by forming the clay by pinching, rolling, cutting, carving, and adding sections, you will have to follow the several drawings as a guide for your eyes and hands.

2. First, make an egg shape, 2 inches long—the widest end will be the front of the cock's body. At what will be the lower side, use the plastic tool and wire modeling tool to scoop out some of the inside clay so the body will dry out before baking.

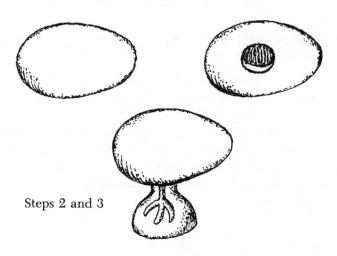

Steps 2 and 3

3. At the bottom of the egg shape add a bowl-shaped lump of clay for a pedestal. Three coils of clay are added on each side as feet.

4. Roll out a slab of clay, ¼ inch thick, following directions in Chapter 3. Set the slab aside to stiffen enough to be handled.

5. For the neck and head, make a tapering coil of clay about 2 inches long and 1 inch in diameter, following directions in Chapter 3. Attach the coil to the larger end of the egg shape, smoothing it into the rooster's body; pinch the body into a pointed curve at the center front. (Some roosters have a flower shape of raised clay on their chests.)

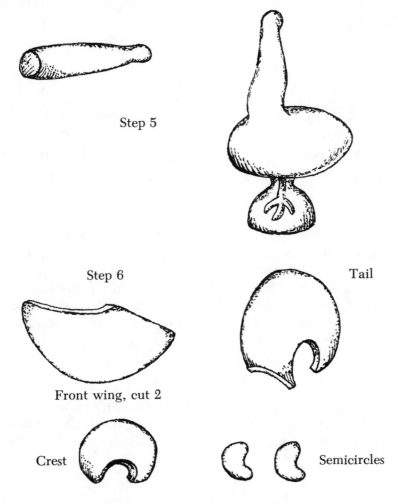

Step 5

Step 6

Tail

Front wing, cut 2

Crest

Semicircles

6. Cut out pieces of the rolled clay to form the two wings, tail, crest, and two semicircles under the beak. Attach these pieces with slip and thin coils of clay where necessary. Cut notches on the edges of the tail and crest. See drawing.

7. Form the pointed beak, round eyes, and teardrop-shaped lumps below the eyes. Add these shapes to the cock with slip.

8. Let the cock stand until leather hard, then scoop out some of the clay from the inside of the pedestal, leaving a ⅜-inch wall. Add a coil of clay around the bottom of the pedestal. Smooth all surfaces with the damp sponge and wire modeling tool. Let the cock dry completely over several days.

9. Bake the rooster in the oven, following the directions in Chapter 4.

Step 10

Tail decoration,

white with blue triangles

Wing decoration, white stem,

blue flower, white center

10. When the cock has cooled, cover the surface with red color using the flat brush. Let dry. Add the decorations (see drawings) of blue and white with the round #4 and #2 brushes, and let the color dry. Follow directions for glazing or painting in Chapter 4.

11. If you have used acrylic paint, cover the outside surface with acrylic polymer gloss medium, and let dry. The air-dried glaze will not need this extra coat.

CAUTION: Make a ¼-inch hole on the top of the cock's body between the neck and the tail, so the air inside can escape as it heats up and expands during baking—otherwise the cock will shatter.

United States

EARLY AMERICAN CANDLE HOLDER

From the end of the eighteenth century to the present day there have been potteries in the Bennington area of southern Vermont. Early on, a type of mottled glaze came to be known as Bennington Ware. There were many forms of pottery including hand-warmers in the shape of books, pitchers, candle holders, covered jars, bean pots, sugar bowls, as well as many other household wares.

Their basic glaze color was a deep cream with mottlings of brown, known as "tortoise shell" pattern, as well as spatterings of blue or other colors against the cream background, and, at times several colors formed the patterns.

This candle holder base is made from a slab of clay, draped over a saucer, with holder and handle formed from flat strips of clay.

Materials and Tools
ruler
oven-baked clay, approximately 1 pound
saucer 5¾ inches in diameter
tools and other supplies (Chapter 2)
candle, ¾ inch in diameter, 6 inches long
air-dried glaze or acrylic paint, white, chrome yellow,
    brown (or color of your choice)
acrylic polymer gloss medium
flat, ¾ inch wide, and round #4 watercolor brushes
    (for air-dried glazes)
flat, ¾ inch wide, and round #4 nylon brushes
    (for acrylic paints and medium)

Directions
   1. First, read the directions in Chapter 3 for making a slab plate.
   2. Prepare the saucer mold. Roll out a 6 × 9-inch slab of clay, ⅜ inch thick. Cut out a 6 × 6-inch square of clay and drape it over the bottom of the saucer.
   3. Curve a coil of clay, ⅜ inch in diameter into a 2-inch circle in the center of the clay saucer as a foot (see drawing).
   4. Allow the clay to partially stiffen, then remove it from the mold. Turn the saucer-shaped clay right side up.
   5. Cut a strip 3¾ inches long and 1½ inches wide from the remaining clay slab for the tube candle holder. Also cut a strip 6 inches long and 1 inch wide for the handle.
   6. With the 3¾-inch strip form a tube, with an inside measurement of 1 inch, in the center of the clay saucer, fixing it in place

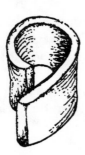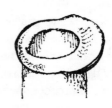

Step 6

with slip and a narrow coil of clay. The clay will shrink in drying, so the tube must be ⅛ inch larger than the candle—all around the inside. Add a coil of clay ½ inch in diameter around the top edge of the tube, extending outward. Hold it in place with slip, and, with your fingers, pinch it into a flat rim, slightly curved upward.

7. Curve the 6-inch strip of clay into the handle (see drawing) and attach it to the upper and lower sides of the clay saucer, using slip.

Step 7

8. Let the candle holder dry until leather hard, then smooth all the surfaces with a damp sponge. Dry thoroughly for several days before baking in the oven.

9. Bake the candle holder in the oven, following directions in Chapter 4.

10. Follow the directions in Chapter 4 for glazing or painting the clay. For the base color, mix a little yellow with the white, and apply to all surfaces of the candle holder with the flat brush. Let dry.

11. When the base color is dry, add the large and small splotches and splatters with the brown color using the round brush. Let dry.

12. If you have used acrylic paint, then cover all surfaces with acrylic polymer gloss medium, and allow the candle holder to dry for several days. Air-dried glaze does not need this extra clear coat.

SOUTHWEST-INDIAN BOWL

The designs on the pottery of the southwest American Indians, living mostly in the Pueblos or along streams, reflect their daily life of hunting, fishing, and farming. Their designs of animal, bird, insect, and plant life are painted in a geometric style. These pots, including bowls, storage containers, and water jugs, were the household wares as well as ceremonial ones, and they were all made from a low-fired terra-cotta clay, and decorated with black and white slips.

This shallow bowl design is from the New Mexico "Mimbres" people, known to have lived from roughly 550 to 1150 A.D.—the name having been given to the group by archaeologists, identifying them with the trees that grew along the stream where they lived.

Materials and Tools
typewriter paper, carbon paper, pencil, ruler
   scissors, compass
oven-baked clay, approximately 1 pound
tools and other supplies (Chapter 2)
flat dish or shallow bowl as a mold, 8 inches in diameter
air-dried glaze or acrylic paint, black, white, rust, or terra-cotta

acrylic polymer matte medium
flat, ¾ inch wide, and round #4 and #2 watercolor brushes
    (for air-dried glazes)
flat, ¾ inch wide, and round #4 and #2 nylon brushes
    (for acrylic paint)

Directions

1. Follow the directions in Chapter 3 for making a slab bowl.
2. Prepare the mold, then drape the clay slab over the bottom, trim the edges, and add a coil of clay curved into a circle in the center of the bowl for a foot.

Step 5   Enlarge to ½" squares

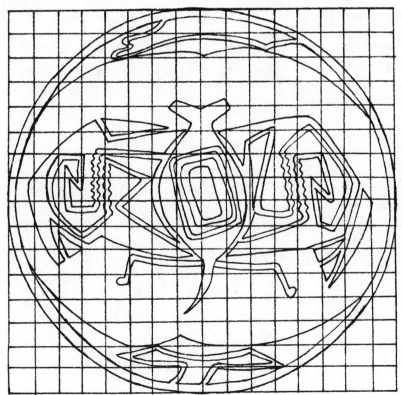

3. Allow the clay to stiffen enough to be removed from the mold, then remove and turn the shallow bowl right side up to continue drying until leather hard. When the clay is leather hard, smooth the inside and outside of the bowl with a damp sponge and the wire tool (see *Variation*).

4. Dry the bowl thoroughly, then bake in the oven following directions in Chapter 4.

5. While the bowl is cooling, enlarge the pattern for the interior design on the typewriter paper following directions in Chapter 2. Transfer the pattern to the dish, using carbon paper.

6. Following the directions in Chapter 4 for glazing or painting clay, glaze or paint the terra-cotta areas of the design first and let dry. Then paint the white areas and let dry. Finally, add the black color and let dry. Turn the bowl over, and glaze or paint the underside with terra-cotta color. Suggestion: you can completely cover the inside of the bowl with terra-cotta glaze or paint, then when it has dried, add the white and black design, and let dry.

7. If you have used acrylic paints, cover the outside and the inside of the bowl with a coat of acrylic polymer matte medium, and allow the dish to dry for several days. Air-dried glaze does not need this extra coat.

Variation

You may want to hang the bowl on a wall as a decoration. Punch a small hole in the side of the foot at the area which will be the top center of your design. Do this when the clay is leather hard, using either a thin skewer or nail. Be sure to check the hole's position before transferring the design to the bowl. When the bowl has been decorated and is thoroughly dry, pull a length of wire through the hole, twisting it to form a hanging loop.

STONEWARE STORAGE JAR

For more than two centuries from the middle of the eighteenth century to World War I, simple, heavy-walled stoneware jars with deep gray or light brown glazes were sometimes decorated with small blue designs. They were made by potters all over the country. These jars were part of every household—they held pickles and preserves, butter, flour, cookies, molasses—all the foodstuffs that had to be stored in a cool preserving cellar or on kitchen shelves.

In spite of small variations in shape and design, the jars looked pretty much alike with wide mouths and small, looped or shelf-like handles; some had rounded sides, others were straight sided. The twelve-inch-high original of this project jar was made around 1800; it had a medium brown glaze and a design in dark blue. The project copy is six inches high, which is an easier size to bake in the oven.

Materials and Tools

typewriter paper, lightweight cardboard, carbon paper, pencil,
  ruler, scissors
oven-dried clay, approximately 1 pound
tools and supplies (Chapter 2)
skewer, small nail, or round toothpicks
air-dried glaze or acrylic paint, white, brown, dark blue
acrylic polymer gloss medium
flat, ¾ inch wide, and round #4 and #2 watercolor brushes
  (for air-dried glaze)
flat, ¾ inch wide, and round #4 and #2 nylon brushes
  (for acrylic paint and medium)

Directions

1. First, read the directions in Chapter 3 for making a coil pot.
2. Enlarge the template pattern onto the lightweight cardboard following directions in Chapter 2. Cut out the template with scissors.

Template, discard dotted areas

Step 2

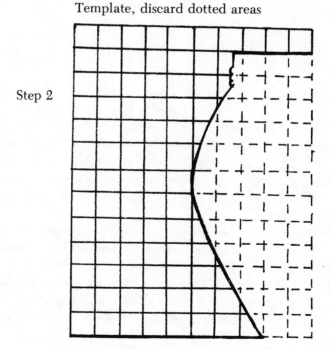

Enlarge to ½" squares

3. Pat out a clay disk 2¼ inches in diameter, and ½ inch thick; center the disk on a plaster bat or tile.

4. Starting on the outside, top edge of the disk, build up the jar with coils ⅜ inch in diameter, checking the shape with the template following directions in Chapter 3. The final jar will be 6 inches high, almost 5 inches in diameter at its widest point halfway up the jar, and the opening at the top is 3¾ to 4 inches wide.

5. With the skewer, nail, or toothpicks, make 4 narrow ridge lines just below the straight-sided top, following the drawing. Also mark a ridge at the bottom of the jar.

6. Form two coils of clay for the handles, ½ inch in diameter, each one 3½ inches long. Add the two coils, on opposite sides of the jar, looping them upward as shown on the drawing, attaching them with slip. Let the jar dry to leather hard.

7. Turn the jar over, and cut a ¼-inch-deep foot on the bottom, following directions in Chapter 3.

8. Smooth all the surfaces with a damp sponge and wire modeling tool, if necessary. Let the jar dry thoroughly for several days before baking.

9. Bake the jar in the oven, following directions in Chapter 4.

10. After the jar has been baked and cooled, mix some of the white color into the brown to make a medium tan color, following directions in Chapter 4 for mixing and applying either air-dried glaze or acrylic paint. Cover all surfaces inside and out with the color, using the flat brush, and let dry thoroughly.

Lion Pattern

Step 11

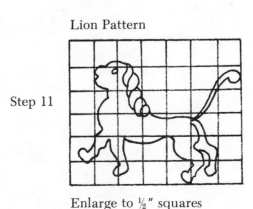

Enlarge to ½" squares

11. While the color is drying, enlarge the lion pattern on the typewriter paper, following directions in Chapter 2 (Enlarging, Reducing, and Transferring Designs).

12. When the tan color is thoroughly dry, transfer the lion pattern with carbon paper to the side of the jar. With the #4 or #2 brush fill in the lion with the dark blue color. Let dry.

13. If you have used acrylic paint, cover the outside surface with acrylic polymer gloss medium, and let dry. The air-dried glaze will not need this extra coat.

Index